Thread

of the

SPIDER

Thread
of the
SPIDER

VAL DAVIS

Thomas Dunne Books / St. Martin's Minotaur ❧ New York

THOMAS DUNNE BOOKS.
An imprint of St. Martin's Press.

THREAD OF THE SPIDER. Copyright © 2002 by Val Davis.
All rights reserved. Printed in the United States of America. No part of this book may be used or reproduced in
any manner whatsoever without written permission
except in the case of brief quotations embodied in critical
articles or reviews. For information, address St. Martin's
Press, 175 Fifth Avenue, New York, N.Y. 10010.

www.minotaurbooks.com

Library of Congress Cataloging-in-Publication Data

Davis, Val.
    Thread of the spider : a mystery / Val Davis. — 1st ed.
      p. cm.
    ISBN 0-312-27681-8
      1. Scott, Nicolette (Fictitious character) — Fiction.
2. Women archaeologists — Fiction. 3. Bank
robberies — Fiction. 4. Utah — Fiction. I. Title.

PS3554.A937836 T48 2002
813'.54 — dc21

                                                2002068377

First Edition: October 2002

10 9 8 7 6 5 4 3 2 1

To David E. Miller

Thread
of the
SPIDER

1

Knute cradled Nora, while she cradled his .45 automatic. Never be caught unarmed, they'd decided the moment they'd gone into business together. She snuggled. He squeezed. The .45 glistened with gun oil.

Lightning flashed, thunder hard on its heels. The morning was dark with the promise of a deeper gloom.

Knute leaned close to the windshield, bringing Nora along with him, to peer up at the Wasatch Mountains, where towering thunderheads were boiling over the sheer eleven-thousand-foot peaks. Near the base of one granite tower a whitewashed Y marked the presence of nearby Brigham Young University.

Dance music on the Packard's radio faded. An announcer said, "This is KSL, Salt Lake City. The massive storm front, which has already dropped more than five inches of rain, is moving south. Flash-flood warnings have been issued as far as the Arizona border. Areas along the Jordan River are being evacuated, and—"

Knute switched off the radio.

"We picked a fine day for it," Nora said, pointing her nose at the First National Bank of Provo across Center Street. Her breath steamed the windshield.

"For luck," she added and kissed the man who had been her lover since high school.

He broke contact, grinning. "You're my luck. Besides, cops don't like getting wet any better than real people. I figure they're all down at the drugstore swilling Postum."

Nora crossed her fingers. They hadn't fired a shot in anger for three bank raids now. For effect was another matter. And they prided themselves on never having killed anybody. Wounded, yes, but definitely not killed.

Lightning lit up the street like a flash camera. Inside the bank, lights flickered.

"That's all we need," Knute said, wiping mist from the rain-splattered windshield. "If the power goes, we'll be working in the dark."

Up and down Center Street, lights flickered in the tidy store windows. There was no traffic on the streets. The shopkeepers who had to be at work were already there. Their customers had more sense.

Knute tapped the dashboard clock. Automobile clocks were notoriously unreliable, but not their Packard. It was the best money could buy. A 1937 convertible sedan, maroon with a V-12 engine whose 175 horsepower could challenge anything on the road. Its luxuries, besides an accurate clock, included power-assisted brakes and clutch.

"Ten o'clock," he said. "Time to go to work."

Knute gave her one last hug before reaching into the back-seat to grab the Thompson submachine gun. Gently, he laid it in Nora's lap as he took back his .45.

She nodded once, then went to work, checking the weapon quickly and expertly. The Thompson was her trademark. When newspapers ran her photo, they invariably picked the one with her holding the Thompson like a baby, while Knute stood beside her, his arm draped over her shoulder like a proud father in a family portrait.

Together, they were a legend in Utah, every bit the equal of Bonnie and Clyde. Their exploits were followed as closely as Joe DiMaggio's batting average. Word was that they'd robbed a hundred banks and were millionaires because of it. In truth, Provo's First National was to be number sixteen. Their last bank, up Highway 91 in Brigham City, had barely kept them in eating money the three days they'd splurged on their way south to Provo.

Some news hawks called the pair modern-day Robin Hoods, stealing only from rich bankers and the hated federal government, hated in Utah since the day President James Buchanan sent an army against Brigham Young and his polygamist followers.

Followers of Knute and Nora said they'd never be caught. Certainly, no true son of Utah would ever give them up, not in this lifetime.

Nora finished her inspection and cocked the Thompson.

"If Mother could only see me now," she said with a wistful half-grin.

Knute started to say something, then thought better of it. Nora's mother had disowned her daughter the day she took up with him.

"We're immortal," he said.

The clouds burst open. The Packard's roof thundered under the onslaught.

"You see," he laughed. "We're home free. No cop ever born would leave his nice, hot Postum on a day like this." Knute laughed in disdain. He was a coffee drinker and looked down on the strict Mormons, whose religion forbade the drink. It was almost harder to buy a good cup of coffee in Mormon Utah than it was to rob a bank.

They trotted across the street, bent over at the waist to keep their weapons dry. A Thompson, Nora had learned from past experience, could be cranky.

The guard opened the door for them. Nora thanked him while Knute was knocking him senseless. A good entrance was important. It kept the customers in line and the guard from causing trouble. Somehow, bashing bank guards didn't hurt the couple's image. Usually it never made the papers.

But today, there wasn't a customer in sight. Just three dispirited-looking tellers and a bank manager in a three-piece funeral suit. No need for Nora to fire her trademark burst into the ceiling.

She eased her finger from the trigger, feeling let down, and herded the tellers toward the open vault. Knute was there ahead of her with the manager.

Just inside the vault stood a metal table stacked with money.

"That's what I call service," Knute said.

Nora had never seen that much in one pile. Neither of them had expected such a haul from a Provo bank. The town, though Utah's third largest, only had a population of about eighteen thousand.

"We should have brought a gunnysack" was on the tip of Nora's tongue when she spotted the black satchel sandwiched between stacks of money.

"Everybody lie down on the floor in the back of the vault," she said, making her point with the barrel of the Thompson. Usually her ceiling burst made the gesture all the more threatening. But even without it, the suckers went down like tenpins.

Nora nodded her satisfaction at them, like encouraging children. It was part of their routine. Bystanders were her job, since the Thompson took two hands.

Knute, with only a .45 to worry about, always worked the cash drawers and vault, though today every dollar had been ready and waiting for them.

Knute glanced inside the satchel, then turned it upside down. Papers spilled out.

His next glance was at Nora, who'd positioned herself so she could watch the door and her tenpins at the same time.

"We're clear," she said. "It's raining cats and dogs out there."

Knute snatched up one of the papers and held it up to the light. From where Nora was standing, it looked heavy and impressive, like a gilt-edged bond.

Knute shrugged. "What the hell. We might as well take

everything." He stuffed the papers back into the satchel and crammed the money on top. "Ready?"

"Ready," Nora repeated, eyeing the vault's ceiling. The exchange was part of their routine. Probably the ceiling was concrete, a foot thick at least. A burst into it might ricochet, killing everybody. She clenched her teeth in disappointment. Robbing the Provo First National was like taking candy from a baby.

2

Nicolette Scott stepped back as far as the slot canyon allowed, a claustrophobic three feet, and peered at the sheer rock wall looming above her. Seventy-five feet up, maybe halfway to the top, she saw her objective, a small cave so deep in shadow it reminded her of a black mouth gaping in the dazzling red Wingate Sandstone.

She stretched her neck and shoulders, trying to work out the kinks in her muscles. Just getting this far had been a bitch, all because of Elliot's Rules. Her father, Elliot Scott, guru of the ancient Anasazi, laid them down with every class he taught and every dig he led. She was violating one of those rules, "Do not climb alone," at this very moment. She didn't see how she could avoid it. Her father was paired with another archaeologist from the University of Utah. They were working Burro

6

Gulch, three slot canyons to the south of her. That left the two grad students who were sticking to each other like glue. She had no idea what they were up to. Talk about feeling like a fifth wheel.

She was only supposed to be conducting a survey of possible sites. Any first-year student could do that. She scanned the crooked canyon, aptly named Boyle's Twist. It was one snakelike bend after another, five feet at its widest, narrowing to shoulder width more often than not.

"Elliot's Rules," she muttered, while eyeing the cave speculatively. There was no sign of the hand- and footholds the Anasazi would have cut into the sandstone a thousand years ago. Wind and rain eroded everything eventually, but here, in a slot canyon like this, heavy rain would come as a flash flood, scouring even the hardest stone. She wondered how the Anasazi had dealt with the ever present danger. They must have had a compelling reason to locate in such an inhospitable place. Did the "ancient enemy," the Navajo translation for the word Anasazi, also have some fearsome enemy?

Lack of handholds proved nothing, except that new ones would have to be cut, but high enough from the canyon floor to keep hikers and relic hunters from reaching them. That was another of Elliot's Rules. "Do not invite the uninitiated to despoil the sites."

In all, nearly a dozen slot canyons fanned out from Baptist Wash, site of an old mining town that had once stood huddled against the base of an immense sandstone reef. That reef, just west of the Henry Mountains in southern Utah, marked the beginning of desert badlands so desolate that map legends bore the warning: CARRY DRINKING WATER IN THIS AREA. The Spaniards who originally explored the area looking for El Dorado had named it the Devil's Door.

Elliot's initial survey of the canyons turned up suitable caves in only four of the deeply eroded ravines. Of those, Elliot thought Burro Gulch the most likely. Not only did those canyons look right, he said, with large, cliff dwelling–size caves, but they had been mentioned specifically in Hyrum Boyle's diary.

Boyle, an amateur archaeologist who devoted all of his retirement years to roaming Utah's vast desert wilderness, had bequeathed his collection of Indian artifacts to the University of New Mexico. There, in basement storage, his diary lay unread until Elliot stumbled across it.

"The canyons nearest Baptist Wash revealed little, but Burro Gulch yielded some promising finds, though there wasn't time to pursue them," Boyle had written. "Burro Gulch, along with several other ravines, were considered sacred by the local Indians. The chief himself once told me that the high caves in there were ancient burial sites and taboo to his people for as long as the sun had set and the stars had shone."

Taboos were a good sign, Elliot preached, because they preserved archaeological sites from the superstitious. He was very excited about the possibility of actually finding a formal Anasazi burial site. None had ever been discovered.

In addition to the diary, Boyle's collection had included some of the finest examples of Anasazi basket work ever found. Unfortunately, Boyle hadn't bothered to label his finds. So Elliot didn't know which, if any of the artifacts, had actually come from the Baptist Wash area, let alone Burro Gulch.

Nick eased off her backpack and sat down to rest, leaning her head against the sandstone wall so she could gaze up at her cave. Hers because Elliot and Reed Austin, the University of Utah man, had both dismissed Boyle's Twist as an unlikely site. It was too narrow and too quirky, just like the man whose name it bore. Besides, Boyle, nicknamed Baptist Boyle, hadn't mentioned it in his diary. A hide tanner by profession, Boyle had ended his days, so legend said, looking for a mother lode that never existed, with only Indian artifacts to show for his efforts.

Nick knew how he must have felt. She'd had the perfect job surrounded by the love of her life, historical airplanes, and she'd lost it. The disaster in Alaska had not been her fault, but she'd been dumped from the Smithsonian. Dumped was her word; staff reduction was theirs. As a result, she'd been forced to take a summer job with her father.

Well, hunting Anasazi with Elliot was a hell of a lot better than spending the summer brooding and waiting for someone to respond to the dozens of résumés she'd sent out. "Wasted paper," Elliot had declared, "since a perfectly good staff position is waiting for you here in Albuquerque."

"Working for you?"

"I *am* chairman of the department."

"Aren't there rules against nepotism?"

"Only Elliot's Rules apply in my department," he'd answered.

Nick smiled at the recollection. She should have said, *two archaeologists in one family was one too many*. Certainly two archaeologists on a dig often added up to one too many. And her presence here brought the count to three, not to mention Reed Austin's kowtowing grad students. In addition, it was never a good idea to have two academic institutions involved in a dig. The politics got too complicated.

Nick lowered her eyes to appraise Boyle's Twist one more time. The canyon corkscrewed so badly she couldn't see more than twenty feet in either direction. Her cave, one of many, had the advantage of being nearest to the canyon's mouth. Beyond it, in the space of half a mile, she'd counted nine more caves, before turning back to get the lightweight aluminum extension ladder, which was rarely used.

With a sigh, she stretched her legs out as far as the opposite sandstone wall allowed. Though she was only five-six, she couldn't straighten her knees. That made Boyle's Twist less than four feet wide at this point.

So maybe Elliot was right. Maybe the Anasazi would have felt as hemmed in and claustrophobic as she did.

She craned her neck. Not a cloud showed in the narrow strip of morning sky visible above. She shaded her eyes and squinted against the glare of sunlight on sandstone, and that's when she saw something. She jumped to her feet and paced, one way, then the other, studying her cave from different angles. Forty feet up from where she stood, what looked like a series of narrow ledges jutted from the cliff face, almost like stepping stones leading to the mouth of the cave. With luck, they'd be wide enough to use as foot- and handholds, though she'd have to move cautiously in case the rock was rotten.

What bothered her was the liplike bulge of stone at the base of the cave. Getting past it would be an accomplishment.

Nick checked her watch. Ten-fifteen, still the cool of the day, though in southern Utah in July, the cool of the morning was in the neighborhood of 85 degrees. God knows what it would be by the time she'd have to lug the ladder back to camp.

"Stop feeling sorry for yourself." The words echoed in the canyon.

She snorted. Sorry wasn't the right word. Foolish was more like it. The climb ahead of her was difficult, not to mention dangerous, thanks to that cave lip.

Nick shook her head. The thrill of the hunt, the prospect of finding an artifact untouched for a thousand years, outweighed the risk. Besides, how many times had she heard her father say discovering an artifact was better than sex? Well, the thrill lasted longer, that was for sure.

In any case, those sandstone ledges were as good as an advertisement that humans had at one time used this cave.

Chances were, the cave wasn't good for anything but bats, anyway, she reminded herself. So why risk it? To prove that she wasn't as useless as she felt. An out-of-work historical archaeologist who'd screwed up her last two jobs, who'd . . .

"Now you *are* feeling sorry for yourself." She laughed out loud. The sound bounced off the narrow walls of the canyon and echoed up the wash.

So start climbing.

Nick weighed the pros and cons of leaving her heavy backpack behind. Her usual equipment had been augmented by additional water and a heavy rope ladder. That much weight would affect her balance while climbing. But in the desert, the rules of survival outweighed even Elliot's code. Always carry your own water. Never depend on finding it.

She raised the ladder to its full extension, then scooped holes in the dirt to place its feet. She moved a few rocks to steady the ladder. All she would need is for the ladder to slip sideways when she was halfway up.

She fished a water bottle from her backpack and drank deeply, saturating herself against the rising heat. Here, in the canyon's shady bottom, it wasn't bad, but she'd be climbing into sunlight. There, the temperature would be well over a hundred.

She pulled on her backpack, ignoring the immediate complaint from her neck muscles. She jumped up and down on the bottom rung to test its stability. With a deep breath she started up the ladder. When its rungs ran out, she went to work, chopping handholds into the red sandstone. Within moments, sweat was pouring down her face, stinging her eyes and half-blinding her.

Elliot's earlier pronouncement goaded her on. *The caves in Boyle's Twist are too small. The Anasazi built enclaves for mutual protection, not single family homes. They weren't suburbanites.*

The moment she cleared the last ladder rung and anchored her toe in the hole she'd just cut, she had to work one-handed, one hand clinging on for dear life, the other wielding the short handled axe. A mistake now and . . .

Concentrate, she told herself. Mistakes weren't allowed, not here. Make one and she'd kill herself, or worse yet lie in a heap at the bottom of Boyle's Twist waiting for her father to come to the rescue.

By the time she'd cut ten handholds, her right arm was shaking with the strain of working above her head. Her left arm was shaking because her fingers could never relax their grip. The backpack didn't help either. Its straps were cutting into her shoulders like knives, and the constant drag of its weight was sapping her strength.

What the hell had she been thinking? If she'd left the pack on the canyon floor, she could have gone back for it once the new hand- and footholds were in place.

She stopped cutting and clung to the cliff with both hands to rest. The idea of jettisoning her backpack was alluring, but accomplishing it without losing her balance was another matter. Nick sighed and looked up. She still had a long way to go. Retreat beckoned. Start over without the pack, she told herself. Or better yet, try tomorrow when you can get someone to come with you.

Done, she decided, and was about to lower her eyes when she spotted a series of indentations, worn shallow by a thousand years of erosion. They led to the ledges she'd seen from the canyon floor.

For once, Elliot, you're wrong. The Anasazi weren't claustrophobic; they were here. All she had to do now was enlarge their original holds.

A surge of adrenaline kicked in. Exhaustion faded and her aches suddenly seemed bearable. More important, her cave wasn't limited to bats. She was following in the footsteps of the Anasazi. Their footsteps became her mantra. With each step she reminded herself that her toes were treading where the Anasazi had trod a thousand years ago.

Five handholds later she reached the first of the ledges. It was much wider than it had appeared from the ground. As Nick perched on it, she realized that the ledges above were actually a series of steps leading directly to the overhanging lip of the cave itself. Erosion had rounded the steps' nosing, but she felt certain they, too, were hand-hewn.

As she climbed them, Nick never trusted all of her weight to any one step. It never failed to amaze her that the Anasazi could make this kind of climb day after day.

The cave's overhang, which had looked impossible from the ground, had deep handholds cut into it. Here, protected by the projecting rock, the erosion hadn't been as severe as on the rest of the cliff face. Here, the hand- and footholds were still useable.

Moving cautiously, testing each hold before putting weight on it, she pulled herself out of the glaring sunlight and into the dark, low-ceilinged cave, wiggling in far enough to be safe. Only then, blind from the sudden change in light, did she risk struggling out of her backpack.

With a sigh of relief, she closed her eyes and waited for them to adjust.

"Shit!" she blurted when sight returned.

There on the wall beside her, H. BOYLE, 1908 #1, was scratched into sandstone wall.

Nick ground her teeth in frustration. Not only had Boyle been there before her, he'd desecrated the site. God knows what other atrocities had been committed. Probably . . .

She caught herself. Chances were that back in 1908 Boyle thought of the canyon as his own private property. Certainly, he hadn't been equipped with a lightweight ladder. So chances were he'd made the entire climb unaided. Maybe the original handholds might still have been useable back then.

Even so, Boyle had made one hell of a climb, unless he'd roped down from the top of the escarpment. Which seemed unlikely, since that approach required a fifty-mile trip over terrain too rough for a road, or even a modern four-wheel drive. Burro or horse would have been Boyle's only option.

Stop, Nick told herself. Do your job. Don't speculate.

She rummaged in her backpack, extracted a small flashlight, and aimed it at the rear wall. Her mouth dropped open.

She lurched to her feet, her exhaustion forgotten once again, and banged her head against the low stone ceiling. She clenched her teeth, waiting for the pain to subside, angry for letting excitement get the better of her.

Elliot's Rules took over, drummed into her as a child and later as a student.

Be calm on site. Do nothing until you survey the situation. Don't move until you know where you're stepping.

She lowered the light from the wondrous wall to check the floor of the cave. A litter of rocks, nothing more. She knelt, sifting with her fingers, feeling for shards, for arrow points, for anything left behind.

Her light followed her fingers, revealing only chunks of sandstone, not a pottery shard in sight.

She sighed. H. Boyle had left behind his name and date. He should have left nothing but footprints.

Bent at the waist, the beam of her light surveying her every step, Nick crept toward the back of the cave. Her sense of wonder grew with each stride.

The cave was almost pie-shaped, with the narrowest point its entrance. As a result, the rear wall was twenty feet long at least, and covered from one end to the other with petroglyphs unlike any she'd ever seen before. The horned serpent at White Rock Canyon, the Anasazi hunter disguised as a deer in the great cave kiva at Sandia Canyon, the Painted Cave with its hundreds of feet of rock art, all paled compared to the wall before her.

Or was that wishful thinking? Would Elliot only shake his head at her ignorance and cite some reference, some locale totally unknown to her?

He was the expert, not she. He was the source everyone cited when it came to the archaeology of the Southwest. Her field was historical archaeology, the study of the near-past. If Columbus had thrown it away, it belonged to her. The refuse of pioneers, even old airplanes whose crash sites had gone un-discovered, those were her kind of artifacts.

Dumpster diving, Elliot called it in jest. Most of his colleagues, and hers, weren't so kind.

Nick wiped sweat from her face, but it kept coming despite the coolness of the dark cave. Her eyes stung, her vision blurred. She dug out a handkerchief and mopped thoroughly to get a better look.

The light flickered in her trembling hands. Individually the petroglyphs would have been a good find. But as a whole? The more she looked, the more certain she was that they were truly unique. That this could be the find of a lifetime.

Yet maybe they weren't Anasazi at all. Maybe they were Fremont. A thousand years ago, the Fremont Indians had roamed much of Utah, while the Anasazi dominated the great rock plateaus of New Mexico. Unlike the Anasazi, the Fremont hadn't built great cliff dwellings. The legacy they'd left behind wasn't as spectacular. As a result, less was known about the Fremont than the Anasazi.

Nick wracked her brain for memories of Elliot's lectures on the Fremont. Square, stylized heads came to mind, the paw prints of a bear, busy scenes mixing humans, animals, and symbols, almost crude by comparison to some Anasazi sites. Certainly nothing like the wall in front of her, yet . . .

A little of both, she decided finally, a mixture of Anasazi and Fremont. Or maybe she was looking at an anomaly. Maybe this artist was an outsider, or . . .

She snorted derisively. Elliot would flunk any student suggesting such a thing. If it came from her, he'd probably retract his job offer.

Deliberately, Nick moved back and forth, studying the wall from end to end repeatedly. War, she concluded at last, she was looking at a depiction of war.

She double-checked the animals on the wall. Strictly food animals, certainly nothing that resembled a horse. A horse would have put an end to her find, since the Spanish had introduced them to the New World long after the Anasazi and Fremont had disappeared.

Nick moved back to the entrance and sat cross-legged, staring at the canyon's opposite wall. Ten feet below her perch, discoloring in the rock indicated the height of some past flood. Not much leeway, she thought. A few more yards of water and her site might have been ruined.

Her fingers traced H. BOYLE cut into the sandstone beside her. What had he thought of the cave? she wondered. Probably he thought the drawings were Navajo, or maybe Ute. Or maybe his only interest in the cave was leaving his mark. She couldn't recall any mention of pictographs in the diary. Like many amateurs of the early twentieth century he was probably only interested in artifacts that he could display or sell.

She knew little of the man, except that he'd prospected for gold, collected ancient artifacts, and given his name to this particular slot canyon. Maybe Reed Austin could fill her in, since Utah was home ground for him.

The thing to do was get Elliot here as quickly as possible. Elliot and Austin both. Let them decipher the wall. After all, she could be wrong. Maybe it wasn't the wonder she thought. Like hell!

She took her disposable camera from her pack and quickly took some shots. "Just in case," she thought. They would take proper pictures later.

She then extracted a trowel from her backpack and went to work in the loose red soil. Bedrock was no more than an inch down. Into that she drove steel pitons to anchor the rope ladder she'd brought along in her backpack.

Driving pitons wasn't exactly site procedure, but this cave was much higher than most, far out of reach of scaffolding, even if it could be brought into Boyle's Twist.

When she lowered the ladder over the side, it came up short of the canyon floor, but well within reach of the aluminum extension.

At the sight of it, she breathed a sigh of relief. Her father wouldn't have to take the risks she had to reach Boyle's #1.

Suddenly, the thought hit her that maybe Boyle might have left his mark in every cave in the Twist, numbering them as he went along?

She shrugged. If he had, he was part mountain goat.

Nick left her pack, stowed well out of the way, and gingerly tested the rope ladder. The pitons didn't so much as creak.

Only when her feet hit the canyon floor did she allow herself to smile in expectation of her father's face when he saw the cave for himself.

3

Elliot took one look at the rope ladder dangling from the cave and sputtered, "Dammit, Nick, you had no right. Climbing alone is too dangerous."

"Is that a thank you?" she said.

Beside her, Reed Austin opened his mouth as if to say something, then appeared to think better of it.

"You told me you were going to survey the canyon, not go climbing," Elliot went on.

"I'm not one of your students, Elliot. I'm a volunteer, remember, and I'm not being paid. And I did survey the canyon. There are ten caves in the next half-mile, all visible from the ground. If they're anything like this one, we've struck the mother lode."

Elliot addressed himself to Austin. "What do you see when you look at my daughter?"

Austin, a big-boned towheaded man

freckled from the sun, rubbed a hole in the zinc oxide smeared along the bridge of his nose and grinned sheepishly.

"Well?" Elliot demanded.

"What he sees . . ." Nick said, pausing to slap the red dust from her jeans, ". . . is a filthy mess who got that way doing her father's dirty work." She started to wipe her face, then figured she'd just be smearing around the red grime.

"That's crap and you know it," Elliot snapped at her. "How many times have I told you: Don't take unnecessary risks."

The trouble was, he was right. Worse yet, she could see that she'd hurt him.

Austin said, "Five-five, I'd guess. Maybe a hundred and twenty pounds. Red hair, at least I think it's red under all that dirt. That's what I see when I look at your daughter."

Elliot glared at him, while Nick, trying to ignore him, brushed at her near buzz-cut, raising a red fog.

"The color's still indeterminate," Austin told her.

"Don't encourage her," Elliot said.

Nick dug her Cubs cap from her jeans and clapped it on tight. "I anchored the rope ladder the way you taught me, Elliot," she said, the start of an apology.

Elliot fussed with the extension ladder, pretending to reposition it. His way of saying, apology noted.

"Maybe I should go first," Austin suggested, smiling crookedly.

"Don't even think about it," Elliot said. "I'm senior here."

Austin snorted. "That's the Professor Scott I remember."

"I should have flunked you when I had the chance."

Austin, who was now tenured at the University of Utah, had earned his doctorate studying under Elliot.

Nick handed her father a coiled rope, which he slung over his shoulder. When he reached the top, the rope would be lowered and they could haul up their backpacks, now heavily loaded with the battery-powered lanterns needed for high-quality photographs of the petroglyphs.

"My God, Nick," Elliot murmured as the first lantern was switched on. "You're right. This *is* the mother lode."

Under bright light, the cave art glowed, as did the surrounding red rock.

"I don't remember seeing anything quite like it," Nick ventured.

"You're damn right," Austin agreed, then caught himself and looked to Elliot for confirmation.

"We shouldn't jump to conclusions," Elliot said. "Something this unique could be . . . an anomaly."

"It could be a fake," Austin said.

"What brings you to that conclusion?" Nick asked.

"No mention in the diary," Elliot muttered.

"On the other hand, it's just possible Boyle saw no monetary value in the pictographs. By all accounts, he sold a great deal of what he found."

"Let's hope that's the case here," Elliot responded.

Despite her father's calm exterior, she knew him well enough to sense his excitement. "And if we find similar work in the other caves?" she probed.

"That's what I'm hoping for."

"It's a good thing you had me along then, isn't it. You might have spent the whole summer in Burro Canyon."

"Don't knock it," Austin said. "There's some good sites there."

"Like this?"

"You know better," her father shot back. "And yes, we're in your debt, and I apologize for being angry. Only don't make any climbs like that again, please. Not without help. Now, if that's settled, I'd like a little peace and quiet so I can study this wall."

For the next half hour, Elliot and Austin went over the petroglyphs inch by inch. Nick stayed out of their way. They were the Anasazi experts, after all, though Austin's last monograph had concentrated on Utah's Fremont culture.

Finally, Elliot said, "Fremont?"

"Their influence certainly," Austin answered.

Elliot nodded. "A mixture then, Fremont and Anasazi."

Austin nodded right back.

Nick smiled to herself. She'd been right after all. *You see, I was paying attention to all those lectures, even when I was a child.*

Elliot knelt in front of the wall. "Like I said, we mustn't jump to conclusions, but this work could answer a lot of questions as to why the Anasazi disappeared. This may be showing us the war they lost."

"It doesn't say who won," Austin pointed out.

"At least we know there was warfare." Elliot shook his head. "Sorry. It's too early to make that kind of assumption."

"It looks like war to me," Austin said. "It would certainly explain why the Anasazi built their cities high up on the sides of cliffs. Of course, some of our colleagues have already suggested they might have been invaded from Mexico by the Toltecs."

"Since the Anasazi and Fremont date from the same period," Elliot picked up, "they could have been fighting over water rights."

A great drought had hit the Southwest in the thirteenth century, Nick remembered. For twenty-three years, no rain fell. The tree rings of the era, 1276 to 1299, testified to the parching of the land.

"Let's pray to God the other caves contain more information," Austin said.

"Another possibility occurs to me," Elliot said. "We could be in the presence of the Anasazi's Michelangelo, or maybe the Fremont's. In which case, we're looking at the vision of one unique genius, not a cultural history."

Nick plunged in. "I think there are at least two hands at work on that wall."

Elliot smiled at her. "Not bad, daughter. That's exactly what I think. And you, Reed?"

"I'd like to think one Fremont and one Anasazi were here working together."

"If the answer isn't here in front of us," Elliot said, "it might be somewhere else in this canyon of Nick's."

"It's Boyle's Twist," she said, "not mine."

"Don't be modest. Reed and I would still be poking around in Burro Canyon if you hadn't gone climbing. If it's all right with you, Reed, I'd like to name this site Nick Scott, site number one."

"Nick's, it is," Austin said.

Nick pointed to the name chiseled in sandstone. "I'm afraid Hyrum Boyle beat us to it."

"He must have been a scoundrel, if you ask me," Elliot said.

Austin snorted. "Remind me to tell you about Boyle when we get the time. I met him once, you know, years ago. I was just a kid. He was one hell of a character."

"Well, his canyon's going to make us famous," Elliot said and grabbed Nick in a bear hug. "What do you say, daughter, isn't this better than finding airplanes?"

Austin looked mystified.

"I can see you haven't been following Nicolette's career," Elliot explained. "Come to think of it, career's the wrong word. Exploits might be better. There's nothing she likes better than an airplane crash."

Austin snapped his fingers. "I remember now. I read about that plane you found in New Mexico."

"It was a B-17," Nick supplied. "Its crew had been listed as missing in action since World War Two."

Elliot pointed a condemning finger. "That's old news. Tell him about your last airplane, the one that damn near got you killed."

"I'm here, aren't I?" Nick spread her arms to prove the point.

"It got you fired," Elliot countered.

"They called it a staff realignment," she snapped, annoyed that her father should be so insensitive.

"Right now," Elliot continued, oblivious to everything but his work, "we'd better realign our own staff. If it's okay with you, Reed, we'll start your students lugging our gear out of Burro Gulch and carrying it over here. We can begin photographing first thing in the morning. When we're done, we'll move onto the next cave." He squinted at Nick. "And no, you're not to go scouting them on your own."

"What am I supposed to do, then, tote equipment alongside Reed's students?"

While Elliot muttered under his breath, Austin said, "You could look for Boyle's gold. They say it's buried around here somewhere."

Inwardly, Nick groaned.

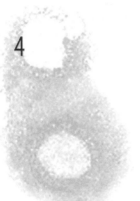

4

Knute couldn't believe their luck. The money on the motel bed came to a little more than twenty thousand dollars. He'd never seen that much before. Hell, not even half that.

"Count it again, Nora." Her eyes were as wide as his.

She licked her lips and went to work.

Tires crunched on the gravel outside, overriding the sound of pelting rain.

Knute drew his .45 automatic with the suddenness of an old-time gunfighter. He stepped to the window and spread a peephole in the venetian blind. "It's nothing," he said, "just Ned going for a drink down at the roadhouse."

"Better he should walk and not get himself arrested for drunk driving."

Knute nodded. "It's a bad night to

drive, that's for sure. I guess our money's burning a hole in his pocket."

"Ned's always been a drinker."

"Never so much I didn't trust him, though."

They'd been holing up at Ned's place, the Manti Motor Court, for the last year, an off-and-on arrangement giving them a hideout whenever they did jobs in the southern part of the state. Ned always assigned them the last cottage in line, the one farthest from Highway 89, with an attached carport that kept nosy cops from spotting their Packard. Of course, they paid through the nose for Ned's cooperation, twenty-five dollars a night. *You're paying for the view*, Ned liked to tell them, *my cottages overlook the temple.*

Knute spread the venetian slats farther apart. The Manti temple's white limestone glowed in the distance despite the downpour. Knute smiled to himself. It was just like Ned to claim exclusivity to a view that could be seen for miles.

Nora clapped her hands. "I was right the first time. Twenty thousand, two hundred and forty dollars. Imagine, a Podunk bank like that having this much cash. God bless bankers, I say."

The money covered the bed from head to foot.

"We'd better stash it, Nora. If Ned gets a gander at that, he'll be upping the price on us." Or worse, Knute thought, but kept it to himself.

Nora fell facedown on the bed, hugging the cash to her bosom. "Now I know what it feels like to be rich." She wiggled in luxury. The sight of her rotating hips aroused him.

"Clear the bed for action," he said eagerly.

She turned over, showering money over the side. "I want to do it this way, lover, feeling the money on my back and you on top." She switched on the radio next to the bed. "Let's have a little music to accompany us."

She fiddled the dial until she found Bing Crosby crooning about love. Knute, his clothes tossed aside, was starting to croon himself when Bing was cut off abruptly.

"We interrupt this program for the following announcement. A statewide manhunt is now underway for Knute and Nora Deacons. The pair are wanted for murder following a bloody bank robbery in Provo this morning."

Knute sat up, Nora right beside him, staring at one another in total bewilderment. The robbery had gone like clockwork, without so much as a shot being fired.

"Two of the dead have been identified as Provo policemen," the announcer continued.

"Jesus," Knute muttered. Nora nodded. Every cop in the state would be looking to get even.

"What the hell is going on?" she murmured.

Knute shushed her.

"The third victim was an innocent bystander," the announcer said. "The Federal Bureau of Investigation has been asked to join in the hunt for these mad-dog killers. The governor has asked that Knute and Nora be added to the FBI's ten most wanted list."

Without a word, Knute and Nora began dressing.

"A five thousand dollar reward for information leading to their arrest has been offered. We now return you to our regularly scheduled program on KOVO Provo."

"My poor mother," Nora said, though she and her mother hadn't spoken in years. "What will she think?"

Knute said nothing because nothing was expected. Instead, he paced, thinking.

At every sound from the highway, he froze, tilting his head to one side to listen like Nipper, the RCA dog. "It has to be the banks," he said finally. "They must have got tired of people protecting us, so they made up this story."

"We've got to tell everyone the truth."

"Tell who?"

"I don't know," Nora said. "Maybe we can start with the radio station."

"Why not?"

The office was dark. So was the rest of the Manti Motor Court. Knute and Nora, its only customers, had switched off the porch lights to keep from drawing attention.

Knute fed the payphone and then had the operator connect him with the radio station.

"KOVO radio," a man's voice said.

"This is Knute Deacons."

24

"Is this a joke?"

"I want to tell my side of the story. Mine and Nora's."

Nora thought that Knute spoke earnestly and even with a touch of eloquence. It didn't take him long, but Nora could tell that he was being listened to. She felt her heart swell. Knute could have been anything he wanted, even president.

Back in their room, Knute and Nora sat in the dark, listening to Glenn Miller's band playing "The Nearness of You." Every once in a while, Knute struck a match to read his watch. Each time he carefully sheltered the flame so it couldn't be seen outside.

Ten minutes passed without another bulletin on the radio. Then twenty. Glenn Miller came and went, replaced by band music from the Coconut Grove.

"They aren't going to tell our side, are they?" Nora said quietly.

Knute clenched his teeth, imagining how good it would feel to shoot up that radio station. Better yet, let Nora's Thompson do the talking for them.

On the radio, the music faded and was replaced by the sound of a teletype machine. "This is a KOVO special report. A man claiming to be Knute Deacons called this station moments ago, bragging about his bloody exploits. He said he and his longtime gun moll, Nora, would shoot down anyone who gets in their way. He then went on to issue the following warning to police. 'We won't be taken alive,' he said, unquote."

"What's happening?" Nora whispered.

Before Knute could answer, lightning flashed, followed by a boom of thunder. In the momentary brilliance, Knute saw the shadow of a man silhouetted against the blinds. Gravel crunched outside, not a heavy sound a tire would make, but the scuffing noise of someone trying to be sneaky.

He touched Nora's shoulder, a warning, then flattened himself next to the door. In the darkness, he heard Nora cock the Thompson. He did the same for his .45.

The wooden stoop outside their door creaked. Ned, Knute

remembered, kept a shotgun behind the counter in the office. A two-barreled bastard that would blow Nora into hamburger if things went wrong.

"Get down," Knute commanded as he stepped in front of the door and fired all eight slugs through the flimsy wood.

The shotgun went off with a thunderous roar, and for an instant Knute couldn't understand why he wasn't dead. His ears rang, but that was all.

He switched on the porch light with his gun-hand and jerked open the door with the other, hoping to catch Ned before he had time to reload. But the only life left in the old boy were twitches, one of which had jerked the shotgun's twin triggers and blown a hole in the porch roof.

Without exchanging a word, Knute and Nora packed their bags, loaded them into the Packard, and drove south on 89. The rain was coming down with a vengeance now, a wall of it that defied even the Packard's high-speed wipers. The headlights couldn't penetrate more than a few yards. Only the white center line kept Knute on course. He drove at a snail's pace, though his foot ached to stomp on the accelerator.

"It's getting worse," Nora said.

"Impossible," he answered, but knew she was right. Highway 89 ran along the great Wasatch plateau, with its granite peaks so high they bred their own thunderheads. He slowed even more.

"Nora, wipe the windshield. I can't see a damned thing."

She used her handkerchief to rub a hole in the mist, but the glass fogged again the moment she stopped.

"Crack your window." Knute rolled down his own and was immediately drenched, but the windshield started to clear.

"This weather's a good omen," he said. "The cops won't expect us to keep moving."

"Only fools would drive in this." She kissed him on the ear. "They say God protects fools."

"God and the Thompson submachine gun."

Nora patted her lap. "Baby's right here."

By the time they reached the next town, Gunnison, they'd

lost KOVO's signal but picked up another radio station in Richfield, to the south.

"The governor has personally doubled the reward for Knute and Nora," the new station reported. "Ten thousand dollars for Knute and Nora, dead or alive."

Nora dialed both ways, looking for another station, but found only static. When she came back to Richfield, it too had faded.

"Turn the damn thing off," Knute said. "We need to think."

"You know what I think. For that kind of money, we can't trust anybody."

"Except maybe family."

"My mother?"

Knute shook his head without taking his eyes from the road. "It's too risky. The cops would be looking for us there."

"Where, then?"

"We'll head south. Across the border if we can. Then we won't have to trust anybody."

"We'll never get anywhere at this speed."

"You're welcome to drive."

"Don't pay any attention to me. I'm just talking. I know you're doing your best."

"Salina's just about fifteen miles up the road," he told her and then shook his head. "That's where I'd be waiting if I was a cop."

They reached Salina at dawn. Knute had timed it that way so he could see what he was getting into. He'd taken the precaution of running without headlights since the last Burma Shave sign.

He braked to a stop on a rise overlooking the town, rolled his window all the way down, and thrust his head into the rain. Nora did the same. Two pairs of eyes were better than one.

There was just enough light seeping over the Wasatch to reveal the sawhorses blocking the two-lane highway ahead. A police car was parked on the shoulder nearby.

"I told you," Knute said. "Cops don't like getting wet. They're inside nice and dry, which means they don't know we're here."

He tapped the side of his head. "They haven't got it up here, not like we do. Now let's crash those sawhorses and be on our way."

Nora wet her lips and cocked the Thompson.

He kissed her, maybe good-bye if their luck ran out, and floored the V-12 Packard.

5

By early evening Reed's two grad students, Art Clawson and Carol Layton, sat slumped in their folding chairs, their heads nodding over their dinner plates. They'd been hard at work for hours, hauling gear from Burro Gulch to Boyle's Twist. As the crow flies the trip would have been easy enough, no more than a quarter of a mile. But on foot, navigating the corkscrewing canyons, each trip was a brutal two miles, Nick estimated, accomplished in 100-degree temperatures.

Watching them poke at their food dispiritedly made her feel guilty until she realized she wasn't doing much better with Elliot's stew. For what it was, right from the can with a little doctoring, it tasted good enough. But Nick's climb, plus the adrenaline overload of her discovery, had left her as limp as Clawson and Layton looked. Whether

her face was as fatigue-gray as theirs she didn't know, but she wasn't about to go looking for a mirror.

With a sigh, she shoved her plate aside. Seeing her jettison the stew, Clawson and Layton exchanged relieved glances, and did the same.

Elliot looked up from mopping his plate clean with bread and said, "My Mulligan takes getting used to."

Both students smiled weakly.

The five of them were seated in a circle. Instead of a campfire, they had a butane stove to stare at. This time of year, with the daytime temperatures blistering, all vegetation was potentially explosive, so open fires were strictly taboo.

They'd pitched their tents on the site of what was once the town of Baptist Wash. These days, there wasn't so much as a chimney standing, although Austin claimed that at one time Hyrum Boyle's shack could be seen, chimney and all. But that, like everything else, had been washed away during the great flash flood of 1993.

Elliot, who was sitting across from Nick, smacked his lips and ladled another helping of stew onto his plate.

Austin, already on his second helping, looked at his students and said, "You'd better eat up. You're going to need your strength tomorrow."

"We'll make up for it at breakfast," Clawson assured him.

Austin chewed for a moment, then nodded. "You two can turn in now, if you'd like. We'll clear up."

The pair fled for their tents before he could change his mind.

"Your stew stinks," Nick said when they were out of earshot.

"It's their first day," Elliot said. "They'll get used to it."

"Crap," Nick said. "I've been there, remember. Summers with the Anasazi. Scorching, blistering, one hundred-degree summers, slave laboring on your behalf. Only melted Milky Ways saved me from starvation."

"You loved it," Elliot said.

"Not the fetching and carrying, I didn't. For you it's the thrill of the hunt. For the rest of us, it was hard, backbreaking work with the constant worry that if you weren't satisfied with our efforts, our grades would suffer."

"I don't remember you complaining at the time," Elliot said.

"Would it have done any good?"

"She's got you there," Austin said. "I was one of those slaves once, remember? Fetching for the great man."

Elliot raised his hands in mock surrender.

"The grand old man of southwestern archaeology," Nick added, "running a sweatshop."

"I may be grand," Elliot said. "But I'm not old. I'm fifty-one."

Nick snorted. "That's not what your birth certificate says."

"Maybe you carbon-date archaeologists like old bones," Austin put in, "with a plus or minus factor of so many years."

"Next time I'll bring my own students," Elliot grumbled.

He was about to say more when the setting sun broke free of the clouds strung along the horizon. For a moment, the sandstone walls looming above them caught fire in the light. Then, just as suddenly, the sun slipped away and the red stone of the Devil's Door ebbed to black.

Austin lit one of their butane lanterns, its hiss the familiar music that Nick had been hearing since her first dig.

"Tell me about Hyrum Boyle," she said, scrunching her shoulders against the sudden night chill. A breeze had sprung up, blowing down from the eleven-thousand-foot Wasatch Mountains northwest of them.

"Baptist Boyle was his nickname. Baptist Wash is named for him, but that wasn't its original name. When he arrived here in the early 1920s, it was called Indian Hollow."

Austin gestured toward the cliffs, now hidden in darkness. "It may not look like it, but Baptist Wash sits in the middle of a hollow, a good half mile long but a hollow nevertheless. It's like the head of a funnel. It catches the flash floods that run off the Wasatch."

In her mind's eye, Nick saw the water boiling against the cliffs, eroding the stone over the ages, carving out fissures that eventually became slot canyons.

"Not the ideal place to build a town," Austin continued.

"But then that was an accident. The place sprang up overnight when gold was found in the eighteen-eighties. Unfortunately, the gold wasn't native to the area. It had washed down from the mountains during the Ice Age, and settled in pockets along the dry riverbeds. It was easy pickings while it lasted, but the boom ran out long before Boyle arrived in the twenties. By then, Indian Hollow had shrunk to a few diehards, and the only gold to be had was from selling liquor to the Indians."

Austin nodded, more to himself than anything else. "A couple of those shacks were still here when I was kid. They were wedged right against the cliff where silt had laid down a bench of high ground over the years. According to Boyle, most of the shacks, his included, had backrooms hollowed right into the cliff, where they could hide their women and booze. Those hollow rooms and their treasures, Boyle told me, gave the town its original name, Indian Hollow. I remember him saying, 'My backroom's full of treasure right now. Boyle's gold.'"

"He was probably making it up," she said.

"Maybe, but Boyle did show me one of the hollow rooms. It was caved in mostly and there was no shack left in front of it. I remember him saying, 'God only knows what treasures are buried in there.' He said if he wasn't too old to prospect, that's where he'd look. I was only a kid, then, so that's where I dug."

"And?" Elliot prompted.

"I did find a treasure, a wagon wheel and some rusty tools. That was the day I knew I wanted to be an archaeologist. We'd come here on a family outing, my parents, me and my brother, and a couple of our friends. That must have been about nineteen seventy-eight, so I would have been about twelve. In those days, there was still enough left of the road to drive in here without a four-wheeler. Of course, all that washed away in the ninety-three flood, even Boyle's shack.

"Anyway, we were pitching our tents when Boyle suddenly walked out of one of the slot canyons. And, before you ask, no I don't remember which one. I do remember that he looked like he was a hundred years old to me, though ninety was probably closer to the truth. He was the color of tree bark, and so bone-thin he didn't look like he'd eaten in weeks. My mother took one look at him and invited him to take a meal with us. I guess he thought he had to sing for his supper, because he started telling us how Baptist Wash got its name.

"It was the gully-washer of nineteen-thirty-nine, he told us. It killed just about everybody in town except him. It came out of nowhere, a flash flood without warning. One minute, Boyle said, he was talking to one of his neighbors and in the next, he was looking up at a wall of water a hundred feet high. 'I was dead,' Boyle said, 'and I knew it. Then the water hit me so hard it knocked me cold. When I woke up I'd washed up on a rock ledge out in Burro Gulch. That's when I knew God had baptized me and washed away my sins.' "

Austin nodded at the memory. "Boyle told me, swore an oath, that none of the bodies were ever found, proving that he was God's chosen. I know for a fact that some of those canyons stretch for fifty miles, so it's no wonder bodies were never found. Hell, finding a body in there would be impossible, assuming there was enough to find. Besides, Boyle told me it wasn't the first time bodies had gone missing after a flood."

He held up a hand as if preparing to take an oath himself. "That's what I remember him saying, practically word for word. Anyway, Boyle said he renamed the town Baptist Wash and it stuck."

"Let's go back to the wagon wheel," Elliot said. "Did you date it?"

"I wanted to take it home, but my father said there wasn't room in the car. I came back to look for it years later, but by then Boyle was gone and so was his shack. But I remembered where it had stood, so I started digging. I found some old bottles and a telegraph insulator. It was a Provo model, dated nineteen-eight."

"I don't remember seeing any telegraph poles around here," Nick said.

"It could have washed in with one of the floods," Austin said, "or maybe Boyle collected them along with his Anasazi artifacts. I got the impression he was a pack rat."

Nick glared at him. "Why do I get the feeling you're suggesting that I dig for your lost childhood?"

"Actually, I had a prairie schooner in mind. Boyle told me he had one stashed in his backroom. He claimed it belonged to a famous pioneer."

"Did he say who?"

Austin touched a forefinger to the side of his nose. "I asked Boyle the same question. And this is all the answer I got." He tapped his nose a second time for emphasis.

"He was probably stringing you along."

"Maybe," Austin admitted, "but I'd swear he had something stashed away. You would have thought so too if you'd seen the gleam in his eye."

"Swell," she said.

"He was a cagey old duffer, that's for sure."

And what about you? she thought, staring at him in the lantern light. A young man, eager to make his mark in the field. Was this just a ploy to get her out of the way? Even so, prairie schooners definitely came under the heading of historical archaeology.

Nick remembered Elliot saying that Austin had succeeded in obtaining a very lucrative grant that would allow him to expand his monograph on the Fremont Indians into a definitive textbook. So his career was already assured.

Nick glared at him. "You're a dead man if you're making this up."

He crossed his heart. Okay, she decided, she'd give him the benefit of the doubt once, at least. Besides, she'd be in the way while they were photographing the petroglyphs. "Do you have any idea where I should look?"

"Absolutely," Austin told her. "I recognized a couple of landmarks when we got here. I'll show you where Boyle's shack stood in the morning. It's flush up against the Devil's Door."

"Wasted work," Elliot said. "The radio says it's going to be a scorcher tomorrow and you'll be working in full sun out there, Nick. Besides, a prairie schooner's not worth the effort unless it's carrying Brigham Young himself."

6

"This is the place," Austin said, kicking the red earth at the base of the sandstone cliff. The sun, just climbing the horizon, already felt warm on Nick's face. In another hour, it would be raising blisters. "That black rock's my marker."

What Austin called a rock was the size of a pickup truck. It was volcanic in origin and not indigenous to the area, but had probably been carried down the canyon during the Ice Age.

"Even the ninety-three flood didn't budge it. But the smaller ones . . ." He indicated the half dozen or so barrel-size boulders strewn in the immediate area. ". . . they're the ones you have to watch out for. They pinball through these canyons like cannon balls when the floods come. If that happens, you don't want to be in their way. But that big boy, there, he's a fixture. Boyle called that rock his anchor."

Austin squinted at the massive stone as if conjuring the shack into view. "Boyle's place was sagging so badly it would have fallen over if it hadn't been leaning against this rock." He drew a line with his boot. "The front of the shack stood right here. It couldn't have been more than ten or twelve feet wide." He stepped off four paces. "It had a lean-to attached, or maybe a ramshackle garage." He stepped off three more. "The lean-to ended about here."

Nick ran a hand over the black volcanic stone. "Are you sure this is the right place?"

"Unless my memory's playing tricks. Of course, it's been more than twenty years, practically the dark ages."

"That's why I became an historical archaeologist," she said. "To most people twenty years *is* like the dark ages. Our heritage is dying."

"Here's your chance, then," Austin said.

Nick retraced Austin's steps along the face of the cliff. When she reached the spot where he'd marked Boyle's lean-to, she said, "Where was Boyle's backroom, behind the lean-to or the shack?"

"He didn't say."

"What was your sense of it?"

"I was a kid, remember."

"You wouldn't be holding out on a colleague, would you?" She adjusted the bill of her Cubs cap to parry the creeping sunlight.

Austin laughed. "Historical archeology is your field, remember? If it isn't at least a thousand years old, I'm not interested. If you don't mind, I'd better get back to the site. Elliot must be frothing at the mouth by now. You're welcome to come back with me, if you think this is all a waste of your time."

"I'm sorry," Nick said. "I ask you to show me the site and then practically bite your head off. The truth is, I'm feeling like a fifth wheel on this dig. I'll stick around here for a while and see if I can turn anything up. You'd better get back to Elliot before he gets into trouble. He can be very impatient."

"Don't I know."

He smiled. Nick thought that the smile transformed his

36

somewhat raw features into a very pleasant arrangement. Certainly not handsome, but something that would wear very well.

"We could dig here together," she suggested.

"Frankly, I'd prefer it in some ways, but the Anasazi are calling to me. In any case, if Boyle's stash is here, you'll find it with or without my help." He turned on his heel and headed for Boyle's Twist.

"I'll name it Austin's site number one," she called after him, "I'll give you credit for the initial find."

Oh my God, she thought. I'm flirting, archaeologist style. She spun her cap around, catcher style to keep the bill out of harm's way, and began probing the silt that had accumulated against the cliff. But the sun-hardened mud was the consistency of adobe and more than a match for her small trowel.

Grumbling, she trekked the fifty yards back to camp and fetched a handpick, not the recommended tool for careful site work, but the silt was like concrete. As an afterthought, she grabbed a ladder, figuring to dig at ceiling height, say eight feet.

Using Austin's guidelines, she picked a point at what might have been the center of Boyle's shack and went to work, probing the adobelike silt. A foot into it she hit sandstone. She shifted her efforts a foot to the south and probed again. That, too, ended in bedrock. Another foot-long shift to the south ended the same way, as did two others.

By then she'd reached the lean-to, at least according to Austin.

"Your memory sucks," Nick told him in absentia, then shook her head to clear the sweat from her eyes.

She checked the sun. It was closer to noon than morning. She fished a bandana from her pocket and tied it around her head to catch the sweat. Her Cubs cap went on top of the bandana to stave off sunstroke. Then she drank enough water to slosh.

Two more holes, she told herself, maybe three. By then it would be lunch time. By then, Austin would be in big trouble for starting her on this wild goose chase.

Her pick scraped against something metallic. She enlarged the hole, being careful not to puncture the metal. Once the opening was the size of her fist, she used her fingers to clear away the clinging red soil.

She'd struck metal, all right, tin maybe. It looked weathered but not particularly rusty. Thank God for a desert climate and a coating of protective silt.

After an hour of steady, painstaking work she'd uncovered enough metal to be certain she was looking at a door that had been sunk flush into the sandstone. She took a break, swallowing down as much water as she could manage. Keep sweating, that was the key. Drinking and sweating.

Nick wrung out her bandana and mopped her face. The slant of her shadow told her noon had come and gone, and with it her usual lunchtime. Her growling stomach confirmed the assessment. Energy bars and trail mix waited in her backpack. Often on digs she ate while she worked, but not in a searing sun like this.

By the time she took shelter beneath the sunscreens covering their camp gear, Art Clawson and Carol Layton were exiting Boyle's Twist and heading her way. She set up folding chairs for three, then settled down to eat. Both grad students joined her looking surly.

"Dr. Austin sent us to help you," Layton announced. Her tone said she considered the assignment a demotion.

"He said you were looking for hidden treasure," Clawson added, his inflection even more acid.

The pair exchanged glances worthy of asylum orderlies.

Nick washed down a mouthful of trail mix. Bless you, Reed, she thought. I'll never think a bad thought about you again. A small voice inside her asked, *Since when did it become Reed instead of Dr. Austin?*

"It's not fair," Carol Layton ventured. "Doctor Scott says Boyle's Twist is the greatest discovery since Chaco Canyon."

"I'm Doctor Scott," Nick responded.

"You know what I mean."

Nick smiled noncommittally. "My advice is to keep up your water intake." She nodded toward the escarpment. "There's no shade out there."

Both of them squinted at the sun-scorched sandstone cliff.

"There's nothing out there at all," Clawson said.

"To the right of the big black rock," she told them.

They shook their heads skeptically. She couldn't blame them. From this distance, her hole looked like a natural cavity in the rock.

"That's silt out there," she said. "A foot thick at least, which means we've got a lot of dirt to move."

They groaned.

"Have you eaten?" she asked.

They nodded, yes.

"Then let's go to work."

Two hours later they'd uncovered a wall of tin sheets the size of a single-car garage. Nick pried up an edge. The sheets, in strips two feet wide, had been nailed into wood, thick and solid by the feel of it. With luck, the metal, in combination with the compacted silt, would have protected whatever contents were on the other side of the door. In fact, judging by the work required to chip away the bricklike soil, Hyrum Boyle's backroom would have been virtually airtight.

Nick smiled and crossed her fingers. Why go to the trouble of hammering tin over a door if there wasn't something inside worth protecting?

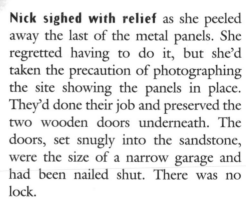

7

Nick sighed with relief as she peeled away the last of the metal panels. She regretted having to do it, but she'd taken the precaution of photographing the site showing the panels in place. They'd done their job and preserved the two wooden doors underneath. The doors, set snugly into the sandstone, were the size of a narrow garage and had been nailed shut. There was no lock.

"What do we do now?" Clawson asked. "Pry it open?"

That would be the quickest way, she knew, but chances were the old wood might splinter in the process. Once that happened, resealing the doors wouldn't be an option. She carefully took pictures of the two wooden doors.

"You two start removing the nails. And be careful. I want the doors kept as intact as possible. And save and tag the nails."

Clawson's shoulders sagged. His cohort, Carol Layton, collapsed onto the pile of silt they'd cleared to get at the door. Red dust streaked their faces like blood. They reminded Nick of newsreels showing exhausted soldiers on the verge of surrender.

There had to be a hundred nails holding the door in place, a good sign that the doors hadn't been exposed to rock hounds or tourists.

"With the three of us working together, it will go a lot faster," Nick said.

"What the hell do you expect to find inside?" Layton wanted to know.

"Why nail a door shut if you aren't protecting something valuable?"

Layton perked up. "That makes sense."

Boyle had ranged this area for years collecting any Indian artifact that he could carry. The museum had many examples of pottery that he had sold to make a living. What if he had held his choice finds back? Wouldn't that be a joke on Dr. Reed Austin.

"We heard Dr. Austin say something about Boyle's gold," Carol said.

"That's the great thing about digs," Nick answered. "You never know what you're going to find."

They exchanged eager glances and went to work on the nails.

Nick felt a momentary stab of conscience for stretching the truth. Chances were the only gold in this desert was in Elliot's teeth. Which any self-respecting grad ought to realize, since most digs were little more than exercises in earth moving.

Still, pulling the nails made her fingers tingle in expectation.

8

The Packard's V-12 engine screamed in second gear. The speedometer needle hit fifty. Ahead, the sawhorse barrier, glimpsed briefly between each wiper swipe, grew larger. Rain flew in through the open windows on both sides of the car.

From the engine pitch, Knute knew it was time to shift into high. But the asphalt was glass-slick. The rain was like a fire hose on the windshield. Taking his hand from the steering wheel to shift might kill them both.

"Shift into high for me!" he shouted over the V-12's shriek.

Nora obliged.

The Packard shot forward.

Out of the corner of his eye, Knute saw Nora steady her Thompson on the window sill.

"Hold on!" he said, gripping even tighter against the coming impact.

The huge Packard parted the sawhorses as if they'd been no more than a ceremonial ribbon waiting to be cut.

Knute whooped. Nora cut loose with a long burst from the submachine gun.

Beyond the sawhorses, the road curved sharply before entering Salina proper. Knute eased off the accelerator, knowing better than to touch the brake in this kind of cloudburst. Even so, the Packard skidded briefly on the slick asphalt before he brought it under control.

He let the car coast into town.

"Check the back window," he told her rather than risk taking his eyes from the road.

"Don't worry about those cops. I shot out their tires."

"That's my girl. You hit anything else?"

"Not a chance," Nora said. "I aimed low. If you ask me they were asleep. I woke 'em up, though. You should have seen them tumbling out, trying to get their guns out. I don't think they had time to get off a shot."

"You and me. We're the best." He howled with delight.

Her hand caressed his thigh. "Wait till I get you alone tonight."

"You're making me hungry," he said, licking his lips, teasing. "What do you say? Do you want to stop for breakfast?"

"You think it's safe?"

"We're indestructible, you know that."

She kissed him. "Let's look for a place."

They rolled to a stop in front of the Salina Café, showing no lights inside except a neon Fisher Beer sign.

"We're going to have to wait for them to open up."

"It's won't take those cops long to walk into town," Nora reminded him. "Why don't I make us some sandwiches, while you put some miles between them and us."

"You're on."

While Knute drove, Nora crawled into the backseat where they kept their groceries. "The bread's soggy."

"Just give me an apple, then."

Nora polished it on her sleeve before handing it to him.

"You want anything to drink?" she asked. They had beer and soda.

"I could use a cup of coffee, that's for sure."

"Me, too."

She scrambled back into the front seat, bringing the sack of apples with her.

"The next big town is Richfield, the county seat," Knute said between bites. "We'll stop there for coffee and gas. We'd better check the radio though, just to see what the hell the cops are up to."

With a nod, Nora switched on the radio, already tuned to the Richfield station. The sweet sound of Morton Downey lit up her face.

"No news," she said. "We must have outrun them."

Knute glanced at the dashboard clock. "We're coming up on the hour. We'll know then."

The hour came and went with only a station break before Morton Downey picked up where he'd left off. By then, the rain had eased enough so that Knute put his arm around Nora and hugged her to him while he drove. They snuggled and sang along at the top of their lungs.

Downey faded away and an announcer came on to invite his listeners to join him at the We-Ask-You-Inn Café for the best home cooking in Richfield, fried chicken a specialty.

"Sounds good to me," Knute said.

"I'll settle for bacon and eggs," Nora said.

"Bacon and eggs *and* fried chicken." He squeezed her. "With you as dessert."

Morton Downey came back.

"You took the words right out of my mouth," Nora said.

Her hands were starting to get frisky when the announcer broke in. "We interrupt our regular program for this important announcement. There's been a massacre just outside the town of Salina. Police say Knute and Nora Deacons crashed through a series of roadblocks, machine-gunning innocent women and children as they made their bloody escape. All of southern Utah has been put on alert."

Knute ran off the road, sliding sideways on the muddy shoulder before fighting the Packard to a stop.

"What the hell is going on?" he shouted at the radio.

"It's the bankers," Nora said, her voice stretching thin. "It has to be."

Knute pounded his fist against the steering wheel. "Maybe it's the cops, making up lies about us. Maybe they're tired of us making them look like fools."

"We haven't killed anybody," Nora said.

"You're forgetting Ned at the motel."

"He doesn't count."

"Tell that to the cops."

Tears welled from her eyes. "We've got to get off this highway."

Two towns later, at Sigurd, known for its gypsum mines, they turned east on State Highway 24 and headed into the badlands.

"Are we going to see your cousin?" Nora asked, sounding like herself again.

Knute nodded. "He's kin. We can trust him."

"With ten thousand on our heads?"

Knute thought that over for a while. "We'll cut him in for a share. That way he'll stay loyal."

"Sounds good."

"We'll stash the car and the loot, borrow Boyle's truck, and head east into Colorado until things cool off. We'll borrow some of his hayseed clothes, too, and disguise ourselves."

"And after Colorado?"

"Then, Nora, we'll come back for our money and retire. Maybe buy a ranch."

"And have kids."

"Anything you want, darlin'."

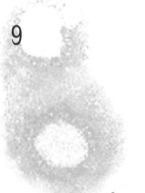

9

Once the nails were pulled, each squeaking in protest, Nick sprayed the hinges with WD-40, then inserted a slim crowbar into the narrow crack between the doors and applied gentle pressure. The doors didn't budge, but one of the hinges cracked ominously.

She immediately withdrew the crowbar and went back to work with WD-40, this time saturating every inch of the rusted metal. If that failed, she'd have to try removing the screws to the hinges.

Wishing for shade, she collapsed cross-legged onto the red ground and waited for the WD-40 to go to work. Clawson and Layton stayed on their feet, staring at her as if assessing her mental stability. After a moment, they joined her on the scorching sand.

Nick scanned the sky, hoping for clouds, but even the distant Wasatch

Mountains dazzled in clear air. The temperature in the sun was over a hundred.

She wet her cracked lips and muttered, "To hell with it. "Let's break in if we have to."

You're flunked, her father would have said.

But the last dose of WD-40 had done the trick. One of the doors gave way, exposing a rock cavern cut into the sandstone cliff. And there, sunk in six inches of seeped silt, sat a dust-covered convertible, its top in tatters, its tires long since flat and disintegrating.

"I'll be damned," Clawson said and started forward with Layton right behind him.

"Hold it," Nick commanded. "We'll open the other door first."

Ten minutes later, with the cavern fully exposed, Nick knelt at the back of the car and ran her gloved hand along the rear bumper, revealing the corroded but still recognizable Packard emblem. Her hand trembled as she edged around the driver's side of the car, her back scraping the cave's rough-hewn sandstone wall. One look at the radiator told her what she already suspected, that she was looking at a 1937 or '38 Packard four-door convertible.

She wiped a peephole in the dusty window. The car's interior, despite the disintegrating top, appeared to be in reasonable condition.

The makeshift garage was no more than a foot wider than the car itself, which left her with maybe ten inches of maneuvering room on the driver's side. There was barely an inch or two of clearance on the passenger side.

Nick wriggled her way back to the rear bumper where she squatted next to one of the chrome-plated wire wheels.

"Refresh my memory," she said without looking at the grad students, both of whom attended the University of Utah. "Were there any halfway decent roads in the area, fifty years ago?"

They both shrugged.

Layton said, "A lot of roads have washed out over the years. Why are you asking?"

Nick ran her fingers over the wheel's hub, clearing sixty years of accumulated dust from the red lacquered emblem.

What would a prospector want with a high-performance car like this? She tried to imagine a man like Boyle driving into town dressed in his Sunday best behind the wheel of the Packard. The image seemed more natural associated with speakeasies, Prohibition bars run by gangsters. Utah had always been a dry state, perhaps bootlegging was another sideline of Boyle's.

"There's no gold, is there?" Layton said.

From an historical point of view this car was pure gold. But she knew that the grad students were too young to appreciate it. The dusty surface of the huge rear trunk tantalized her.

She took a deep breath. "There's only one way to find out."

10

The trunk was locked. Nick fought an overwhelming urge to pry the lid open. Okay, she thought to herself, we've spent too much time in the sun.

"All right, boys and girls, let's take a break. I bet Dr. Austin will be thrilled with your work on this piece of history."

The students eyed her with disdain.

"I'm sure you're anxious to get back to the main dig. Let's go see what they're up to."

It was a relief to walk in the shade of the canyon walls. They met her father and Austin on the way. Just as she was about to tell Elliot about her prize, Elliot insisted on dragging her back to yet another Anasazi find, a much larger cave than the first one she'd discovered. The new cave, like Boyle's #1, had impressive petroglyphs, but what excited her father and Austin was the stone wall at the back of the rock chamber.

As Nick stood looking at that wall, still breathless from the climb, she thanked God this cave was only forty feet from the canyon floor. Because of that her father had made the initial climb himself, with little risk. This one also had an inscription scratched near the red rock opening. H. BOYLE, 1908, #3. "Forty feet can still kill you," she reminded him.

"Look at the wall and tell me what you see?" Elliot responded impatiently.

Nick grabbed one of the battery-powered lanterns and stepped close. "Good craftsmanship dating from the Pueblo Two period, maybe Three. About twelve hundred A.D. The end of the empire, so to speak."

Elliot snorted his approval.

Austin chimed in. "With an eye like yours, Nick, you're wasting your time with airplanes."

It's better than walking in my father's shadow, she answered to herself.

"Don't waste your breath," Elliot quipped. "My daughter's a lost cause. A born trash picker, one step up from a Dumpster diver."

"If that's the case," Nick shot back, "why am I here and not with my Packard?"

Her statement had the desired effect.

"What Packard?" both men said almost in unison. Austin, made the connection faster.

"Boyle had a Packard?" he asked.

"Not just any Packard," Nick replied. "A four-door convertible. Looks like a powerful machine, too."

"Well I'll be damned. I wouldn't have thought of the old boy as the convertible type."

"Why are we talking about twentieth-century artifacts when there's a tunnel to dig?" Elliot complained.

One close-up look at the wall told her more than a tunnel would be needed. The stone slabs, fragile enough on their own, were stacked and interlaced like bricks. Remove the wrong one, or any one for that matter, and the whole structure might collapse. Any kind of opening would have be shored up as they went along.

"What about Layton and Clawson?" she asked, dreading the slow, tedious work, but knowing she'd have to give in to her father's request.

"They're good," Austin said. "But not experienced enough."

"We can't risk a find like this." Elliot wielded his lantern beam like a lecturer's pointer, highlighting one petroglyph after another. "This cave is unique. The entire canyon is. So who's to say what's behind that wall, maybe the answer to the Anasazi disappearance, maybe proof that the Toltecs joined forces with the Fremont Indians in a great war, forcing the Anasazi to fight on two fronts."

Elliot smiled sheepishly. "And maybe there's nothing at all behind it. But we can't take the chance of using inexperienced diggers."

"Students learn by doing," Nick pointed out, "just like I did."

Elliot shook his head sharply. "Fame and fortune could be a wall away."

She'd heard it before, the carrot he'd always dangled to keep her working like a slave.

"My Packard is here and now. And I've still got the door locks to tackle. I need to get inside that car without causing any further damage."

"It's the same with our wall," Elliot countered.

Austin held up a hand like a peace negotiator. "Your father's right about this canyon. Every cave has to be explored eventually."

"That's going to take all summer."

"Help us with the wall and we'll owe you," Austin said.

"Do you pick car locks?"

He spread his hands, palms up. "Sorry."

Nick relented just as she knew she would. The Packard, safe where it was, could wait.

Elliot handed her a trowel and a small pick.

"Don't look so smug," she snapped at him. "Whatever we find, it won't be proof, only theory. Petroglyphs, no matter what they depict, will never provide conclusive evidence of what happened to the Anasazi, only good guesses. Whereas my Packard has a written history to go along with it."

Elliot groaned. "That car of yours won't be a true artifact for another thousand years. So take my advice. Rebury it and leave instructions that it's not to be opened for another millennium."

"Laugh all you want, but that Packard's mine. You two can keep your nameless Anasazi, I've got Boyle's 'treasure.' "

"Treasure like that is one step up from litter," Elliot complained. "Unravel the mysteries of the past and you have pure gold."

11

Ahead, a shaft of sunlight broke through the overcast. Where it touched the desert floor, the red soil seemed to catch fire.

Knute took it as a good omen. Not only had the rain stopped, but they hadn't seen another car since turning off Highway 24 onto Notom Road. Even the towns of Notom and Hanksville, decimated by the Great Depression, showed no cars on the street.

Back in the 1890s, Knute remembered hearing, Hanksville had been a rendezvous for the Robber's Roost gang. Back then, the locals had sheltered Butch Cassidy and the Sundance Kid, who had preyed on the big cattle companies just the way Knute and Nora preyed on banks.

Another shaft of sunlight stabbed the desert to the south, then another.

"We're heading into sunlight, baby," Knute said.

Nora pointed straight ahead. In the distance, the great red rock reef that marked Baptist Wash glowed in full sun. They'd outrun the storm front.

"We've done it," she said. "We're safe."

"Not yet, not till I see the look on my cousin's face. If he's going to cross us, I'll know."

Nora cradled the Thompson, freshly cleaned and oiled since being fired outside Salina.

He handed her his .45, which she checked expertly before sliding it back into his shoulder holster, taking the opportunity to caress his chest with her nails.

He blew her a kiss. "Just you wait."

A half mile from the reef, the asphalt ran out, replaced by washboard ruts. Knute slowed to a creep, then allowed the Packard to coast to a halt. Without a word, they got out with the engine idling. The only sign of life was a single spiral of smoke wafting from Boyle's shack. There were no cars to be seen, no movement.

Knute kicked at the sandy soil. There wasn't so much as a tire mark showing. But then the desert wind could cover an army's tracks if it started blowing hard enough.

"Stay with the car," Knute said. "I'll go on ahead and take a look-see. If you hear shots, get out. Save yourself."

"No, I go with you. If there are any shots to be heard, it will be my Thompson singing."

"The cops could be waiting for us," he said.

"If they are, we're dead anyway."

He kissed her. "All right, let's go see if Cousin Boyle has sold us to the bankers."

Boyle took one look at them and said, "I figured you two to be dead by now."

The scowl on Melba's face said she'd been wishing for just that. But Knute didn't count Melba as family, since she was Boyle's common-law wife only. They'd been married for years though, long enough to have three children. The kids had been playing cowboys and Indians the last time Knute saw them, but that was years ago.

"How are the kids?" he asked, being friendly but also wanting to know just who was around. Nora felt the same judging by the way her Thompson was still in a cradling position and ready to have its say.

"Up and left us for the big city," Melba said, her hands on her hips.

"Price," Boyle clarified.

Knute whistled. Price, a hundred miles to the north, had five thousand people these days, with its coal mines and gambling parlors pulling them in like magnets.

"Left me with all the work," Melba said. "Cooking and cleaning while Boyle here is out poking his nose in old Indian caves and digging for treasure."

"You can stop digging," Knute said. "We've brought the treasure."

Boyle closed one eye down to a squint. "What's that supposed to mean?"

"I've got a proposition for you, but first we could use some food."

Melba shook her head, condemning the lot of them. "What else is new? Nobody gives a thought for how hard I have to work."

"Come on, Mother," Boyle said. "The stew's on the stove already." He switched the squint from one eye to the other. "I shot a rabbit for the pot first thing this morning."

"And who had to skin it?" Melba complained.

"I'll give you a hand with the food," Nora said, lowering the Thompson.

"Nothing much to do but set the table, if you can call it that."

Famished, Knute and Nora had two helpings, plus a can of peaches each for dessert. When the last of the syrup had been drunk, Knute leaned back in his chair and sighed contentedly.

"Now about that proposition," Boyle prompted.

"I'll need your word that you won't go after the reward."

"What the hell are you talking about? I ain't heard about any reward."

Knute looked around the shack. "Don't you have a radio?"

"The kids took it with them," Melba answered, "and Boyle's too cheap to buy me a new one."

"There's nothing on it worth listening to anyway," Boyle said. "You can only get the one signal at night."

"We've been on the radio," Knute told them.

Boyle sucked his teeth. "And I'm a monkey's uncle."

"It's true," Nora said. "For robbing a bank."

"Why would they put you on the radio for that?" Boyle asked. "You've been doing it for years."

Nora said, "They say we killed people, but it's a lie. A damn lie."

"Why would they lie?" Melba said.

"We figure the bankers must have got together to stop us robbing them."

"What kind of reward?" Melba asked, her eyes narrowing, showing dollar signs, Knute figured.

Knute held up five fingers, made a fist, and held up five more. "Ten thousand."

Boyle whistled. Melba's eyes bugged out.

"I'll need your word that you'll keep quiet about our visit," Knute said.

"You have it," Boyle answered without hesitation.

"That was fast."

Boyle tapped the side of his head. "Just smart. I wouldn't want the likes of you coming after me. Isn't that right, Mother? We wouldn't want that."

Melba looked from Knute to Nora and back again. "I want to keep on breathing, if that's what you're asking me?"

"Now, Mother. Let's not forget. Knute's kin. Besides . . ." Boyle made a show of putting his right hand over his heart. "You all know God touched me. Since that day, I've kept my sins to a minimum."

When Nora looked skeptical, Melba said, "He's talking about the flood. I was up in Price at the time."

"A wall of water a hundred feet high took me," Boyle said.

"It was fifty the last I heard you tell it," Melba said.

"God reached down and saved me from the flood," Boyle went on. "Baptized me then and there."

"Sure," Melba muttered. "A regular Noah."

"I'm just saying God reached out to me and I took his hand. Since then I'm a changed man."

Melba rolled her eyes.

Boyle crossed his heart. "I'm giving you my word, Knute. I won't give you up."

Knute turned his eyes on Melba. His stare was enough to have her hastily crossing her heart.

Knute nodded, satisfied. "You still have your old Ford?"

"The last time I looked."

"We're going to leave the Packard here."

"A swap?"

"Use your head. The Packard's as hot as we are. We'll stash it in that mountainside safe of yours. Where you stashed booze during Prohibition."

"That was back when they called me Black Boyle, before God baptized me." Boyle shook his head. "About the Ford, though. This is bad country to be on foot."

"You've still got your mules, don't you."

Boyle shrugged. "For what they're worth."

"All right then," Knute said. "What would you say to five hundred dollars for the Ford?"

"Hell," Melba blurted, "with all his treasure hunting, Boyle's never seen that much money."

"Five hundred right now," Knute clarified. "Enough so you can buy yourself another car."

"Two cars," Melba put in. "I'm tired of being stuck here whenever you take off, Boyle."

"And when we get back," Nora said, "we'll cut you both in for a share from the bank."

"How much?" Melba said.

Knute looked to Nora, who nodded. "A third," he said, "a third of twenty grand."

Boyle rubbed his hands together and said, "Let's get to it, then."

Melba's eyes closed to slits, but not before Knute saw greed light them up. "When do we get our share?" she asked.

"We'll squirrel most of it here," Knute said, "except for eating money. When things cool off, we'll come back and divvy up the rest of it. Until then, nobody touches it. Understood?"

Boyle nodded. "Leave it to me. I'll deposit it in one of my personal banks. You never know. As dumb as they are, the cops might come sniffing around."

Knute snorted. "You and your banks. I used to sneak into a couple of them when I was a kid. The ones I could get to."

"I know."

"I thought I was being sneaky."

Boyle tapped the side of his head. "You can't outsmart a man who's been baptized by God himself."

"Deal," Knute said. They shook hands on it. "We'll need some of your clothes, too, yours and Melba's."

12

It took the better part of a day to bore an igloolike tunnel in the rock wall. The opening was just large enough for a person to crawl through. Even so, they'd had to cannibalize several camp chairs and two aluminum cases for shoring material. Any larger a hole would have meant taking a trip to a lumberyard for proper timbering, and the nearest was hours away, much of it on dirt roads.

Elliot, pushing a lantern ahead of him, was the first to crawl through.

"Kiva," he called back.

The kiva, or pit house, was the religious center of Anasazi life. Usually they were dug into the ground, except in caves where deep digging was impractical. By 1200 A.D., kivas had become quite stylized, with six stone pilasters supporting the structure. The interior walls were plastered with clay and painted with sophisticated murals.

Austin went next. Nick stayed where she was. In case of cave in, someone had to be able to go for help.

"Well?" Nick shouted through the shallow opening.

"Reasonably intact," Austin called back. "Shove another lantern through."

Nick obliged.

"Six pilasters," Elliot called out for her benefit. "Definitely Pueblo Three."

Nick kept her ear to the opening, waiting for more, but all she heard was murmuring. A moment later, Austin's head reappeared. She backed up, thinking he was coming out, but he stayed put with just his head showing. Red dust mixed with sweat made his face look gory.

"We'll need to photograph everything before we disturb the site."

"Is that your way of saying I'm not welcome?" Before he could reply she said, "I know. You're only the messenger. Elliot's Rules are now in effect. Avoid site contamination. Keep your crew to a minimum, no extraneous personnel even if they have done all the hard work."

"Sorry."

"So tell me, are there murals inside."

"Yes, and they're perfectly preserved."

"And is the great Anasazi mystery solved at last?"

"It's too early to say, but your father wants to do the photography immediately."

"It'll be dark in an hour."

"You know Elliot."

"Remind him of Elliot's Rule number twenty-two. Don't climb at night."

He stared at her as if waiting for a punch line. When none came, he backed out of sight.

Within seconds Elliot shouted, "Dammit!" and crawled out to meet her, coming to his knees in front of the opening and thereby blocking Austin's exit. "Your mother used to do that, quote me to prove me wrong. Careful, or you'll end up just like her."

Nick's breath caught in her throat. The impending explosion must have shown on her face, because her father looked repentant and said, "You're nothing like your mother. It just slipped out."

Half her genes came from Elliot. Half of her was just like Elaine. The question was, had she inherited her mother's dark half?

"Elaine would have liked your kiva," she said. "The perfect place to hide."

Elliot blinked in surprise. Usually, the subject of Elaine was strictly taboo between them. He wet his lips as if preparing a response, then shook his head.

"Dark places. She liked hiding in dark places," Nick reminded him. Closets, behind the sofa, like a child hiding from reality.

"She said I was the crazy one in the family," Elliot said. "She said my love of dead people was proof."

"Coming through," Austin called, his voice muffled by Elliot's backside.

Elliot touched his daughter's arm, an apology of sorts, and whispered, "Elaine always said, 'She's your daughter. She'll abandon me just like you do.'"

He moved aside, clearing the way for Austin to come through the opening in the wall.

"She was right," Nick said. "I left as soon as I could."

She'd begun by running away at five, though it took her another ten years to make a successful escape. She'd dreamed of flying away in one of her model airplanes, but she took the car instead—Elaine's car after she'd hot-wired it. Elliot had bailed her out of jail.

13

The next morning Nick went back to the Packard, sliding her way along the driver's side until she was facing the door with her legs crammed underneath. In that position, with the cavern's rough-hewn rock wall at her back, she had only inches of work space as she probed the door lock with a dentist's pick, standard equipment for an archaeologist in the field. Her alternative was to use a wire coat hanger, definitely not standard issue, and grapple for the interior door lock button. To do that, however, she'd have to insert the wire between the glass window and the convertible's dilapidated cloth top. And that, she told herself, would be a last resort.

"Who'd bother locking a car inside a locked garage?" she complained aloud.

Thank you, Hyrum Boyle, she answered to herself.

Sweat ran into her eyes, blurring her vision, though she was working blind anyway because of the close quarters.

Her eyes began to itch. She blinked, then squeezed them shut, but that didn't help. The urge to rub them became overwhelming, but her hands were filthy, a mixture of red dust and oil from the WD-40 with which she'd saturated the lock.

She dropped the pick. Groping in the dirt added grit to her fingers.

"Shit!"

Picking the lock was a long shot at best, especially under such conditions. Her only successful foray into lock-picking had been her mother's car. In that case she'd had a friend, the same one who'd taught her to hot-wire, there to help. And she'd been working in a well-lighted garage, not in a shadow-filled, ovenlike cave.

"That's it," she told the Packard. "You've had your chance to do it the easy way."

She wriggled out from under the car and slowly rose to her feet, grating her back against the cavern wall rather than risk scratching the Packard. The convertible top was going to have to be replaced anyway if the car went to a museum.

She worked a hand into her jeans and fished out her Swiss Army knife, opened a short blade, and gently inserted it between the top's rotting seal and the window. Even the slightest pressure crumbled the rubber, leaving a quarter-inch gap. She ran the blade back and forth until she'd enlarged the opening enough to accommodate her narrow, leather belt. As she fed it through the slit, she thanked God she'd opted for a flat buckle, which looped over the lock button on the first try. The button popped up.

Nick crossed her grimy fingers, a talisman against rust, and tried the handle. The door opened. A tribute to Packard's bygone engineering.

She left the door as it was, ajar, and backed out of the cavern into the ferocious sunlight. Blinded, working by feel, she brushed her jeans. Next, she pulled off her shirt and shook it free of dust and grit. By then her eyes had adjusted to the blinding light. She tugged the soaking bandana from around her neck and wiped her hands thoroughly. That done, the bandana went into her pocket. Then, in bra and jeans, she reentered the cave and eased alongside the Packard mindful of her bare back.

She opened the door as wide as it would go, using her folded shirt as a cushion between the metal edge of the door and the rock wall. She kicked off one shoe and slipped her dust-free foot inside the Packard. Her second shoeless foot came next, resting beside the clutch pedal, as she slid into the driver's seat.

Of their own accord, her hands came to rest on the steering wheel. Her fingers tingled as she imagined herself staring through the windshield, bouncing down some dusty road as the engine roared and the tires complained about the bad surface.

Nick opened her eyes, time-traveling in a blink.

She smiled at herself in the rearview mirror. This was as close to history as you could get. She released her grip on the wheel and checked the passenger seat and floorboards for debris. Nothing but dust, as far as she could see.

She ran her fingers under the driver's seat. Nothing. She leaned over and ran her hand under the passenger's seat. Her fingers touched something that clinked.

She stretched until her fingers closed around a metallic treasure. Her breath caught at the sight of it, a brass .45 caliber shell casing. Perhaps Hyrum Boyle really had been a bootlegger. She could think of no other reason for the shell casing. A .45 automatic was hardly the weapon of choice for a hunter, or an archaeologist, for that matter.

She opened the glove box. A road map, wadded rather than folded, was stuffed inside. When she took it out, a matchbook came with it. The book advertised the Coon Chicken Inn in Salt Lake City, with a grotesque, grinning caricature of a black man's face, as much of a relic of time as any Anasazi artifact.

The glove box also gave up three hatpins and an opened pack of Chesterfields. Nick left them where they were and turned her attention to the backseat. There, she found no litter, only dust. Very inconsiderate. Litter and trash were an archaeologist's lifeblood.

Working slowly and carefully to protect the leather from

further cracking, Nick worked loose the seat cushion and looked underneath, hoping for lost coins or similar-sized mementos. The gods of archaeology smiled. Hidden there was a black leather satchel. Though squeezed nearly flat by the car seat, the bag looked otherwise untouched by time. Even its latch clicked open at the first touch.

Her fingers trembled as she opened the satchel. Inside was a single, yellowed envelope. It was unsealed.

She wiped her hands on her jeans, but they, too, were damp with sweat. She left the envelope where it was, reclosed the satchel, and carried it outside into the sunlight where she slipped on her shirt and headed for camp.

There, dry and reasonably clean, she opened the envelope and carefully extracted a folded piece of paper.

It was a note, printed in pencil, and addressed to a Knute and Nora.

"Thank you," Nick said softly. For her, this discovery was as much a mother lode as were the petroglyphs in Boyle's Twist.

> *Dear Knute and Nora,*
> *I read you was dead but in case you ain't I'm leaving you my marker. I owe you the $20 thousand you left in this here black bag.*
>
> *Melba up and left me. I don't know for sure if she had anything to do with Green River, but just in case, I'm cleaning everything out of the car. I took a look at the other stuff and didn't know what to make but if you went to the trouble of getting it, it must be worth something. So I deposited the whole shebang in one of my banks, #6.*
>
> > *Hyrum Boyle*
> > *Jan 1942*

My God, Nick thought, who are Knute and Nora and what was Green River?

1**4**

Nick traced her way into Boyle's Twist. The canyon floor was in 90-degree shade by the time she reached the base of Boyle's cave #3, where Elliot and Austin were putting in a second day with their kiva. If Boyle was consistent, three caves deeper into the Twist ought to bring her to what he'd called his bank, #6.

Below #3, ladders were in place, as was a rope for lowering artifacts or raising equipment. Nearby, Austin's grad students lay sprawled on the canyon floor looking exhausted, their sweat-soaked hair matted against their scalps.

At Nick's approach, Carol Layton raised her head far enough to shake it. "Your father must be fifty if he's a day, so how come he never gets tired?"

"He's killing us," Art Clawson added.

"To my father," Nick said, "the Anasazi are a drug that keeps him on a permanent high."

Layton wet her cracked lips. "I prefer the real thing."

With a shrug, Nick turned away to shout up at the cave. "Elliot, it's Nick. Talk to me."

After a moment his head appeared. "I'm listening."

"I'm on my way to check out the caves deeper inside the Twist."

"What's up?"

"I'll fill you in at dinner."

"Nick, I know that tone of yours."

"I'm not after your Anasazi, so relax."

"What, then?"

"Something came up in connection with my Packard."

"Take Layton with you."

"I'll be fine. I won't take any chances." She showed him the binoculars hanging around her neck. "It's just a recon. I'll mark the caves as I go." She held up a handful of wooden pegs with yellow plastic streamers already attached. "It will save us time later."

"Then why not have company?" Elliot said.

Because, Nick thought, Layton looked in no condition to keep up. Neither did Clawson.

"You know the rules, Nick. No climbing alone. Agreed?"

"What rules?" Clawson asked quietly, but not quietly enough to keep it from echoing in the claustrophobic canyon.

"Doctor Scott's rules," Elliot shouted at the top of his voice.

"I thought I was Dr. Scott," Nick shot back as she began threading her way deeper into the slot canyon, at times so narrow she had to move sideways like a crab. Getting caught in here during a storm didn't bear thinking about. If the water didn't get you, the pinballing rocks sure as hell would.

She looked at the sky, as much as she could see of it. Not a cloud in sight. But the clouds you could see weren't the ones that killed. It was the thunderheads in the mountains miles away that triggered the cloudbursts.

Relax, she told herself. The temperature had to be over 100 degrees in the sun. What vegetation there was looked on the verge of spontaneous combustion. Here, drought was more of a worry than flash flooding.

At every twist of the canyon, she paused to study the vertical walls through her binoculars. Miss one cave, she reminded herself, and the count would be wrong.

The trick was not mistaking a mere indentation for a cave, something easily done if the cavity was in deep enough shadow.

Twenty minutes in from #3, Nick spotted two caves within a hundred yards of one another. The first in line, #4, was one of the worst climbs she'd ever seen. Directly below its mouth, the sandstone wall not only bulged out like a huge goiter, but was riddled with fractures. There, handholds wouldn't be safe. To reach it, you'd have to climb to one side, where the rock wasn't rotten, then use pitons to anchor your rope, so you could swing into the cave. Not an inviting prospect.

The second cave was just as high, maybe seventy feet off the ground, but had no goiter. Whether the rock was safe she couldn't tell from here.

Nick planted markers, then made a note to show her father the site as soon as she got back. Caves that close together might have connected Anasazi households, if not by internal tunnels, then by exterior scaffolding. Assuming the Anasazi were crazy enough to make such a climb day after day.

Nick shook her head. She couldn't remember a site that treacherous to climb.

After labeling the markers with her pen, she rested long enough to drain one of the quart bottles of water she'd brought along. But instead of lightening her backpack, it felt heavier than ever. Making matters worse, her neck ached from the constant strain of looking straight up. Once, she remembered, she'd dislocated her neck watching a meteor shower, and been forced to wear a wraparound brace for the next few days.

So sit down and rest, she told herself. Take advantage of the blistering shade.

But the lure of Boyle's note kept her moving. If #6 had been his bank, God knew what he might have stashed there over the years.

Ten minutes later Nick ran into a rockfall caused by a gigantic slab of sandstone that had slid into the canyon, creating a ten-foot-high dam of boulders the size of cinder blocks. Behind the dam lay a shallow pool of stagnant water.

Nick was halfway across the pool, ankle deep, when she saw the cave. A hundred feet straight up at least, an arm's reach from where the rockfall had sheared away from the canyon wall. The cave was shaped like a mouth, a four-foot-wide smile, maybe two feet high, like a jack-o'-lantern with red gums instead of teeth.

Boyle's bank #6 if her count was correct. But getting up there was going to be a bitch. The area to the left of the rockfall, where the canyon face remained unbroken, looked as smooth as house stucco. Handholds, if there ever had been any, were long gone. Unless she wanted to cut a hundred feet of new ones, she'd have to climb a jagged chimney that had been created by the rock slide.

She waded out of the pool and picked her way to the top of the rock dam. From there, she covered every inch of the chimney with her binoculars. But the more she looked, the worse it got. The chimney was a maze of badly cracked, rotten rock, a climber's nightmare. The first twenty-five feet, with boulders piled almost like steps, would be easy enough. After that, cracks and fissures would have to serve as foot- and handholds. Just how stable those fissures were, she wouldn't know until she was actually climbing.

If she risked such a climb alone, Elliot would go ballistic. And what if her count was off. If so, the climb would be for nothing.

"Dammit!" Maybe the grinning mouth wasn't Boyle's bank #6 after all. Maybe . . .

"To hell with maybes."

There was only one way to be certain, and that was to backtrack and reconfirm her count. Say an hour each way. Two hours of ninety-degree neck and eye strain. By then she wouldn't have the strength to climb.

"Come on Nick," she said to herself out loud. "You're a professional. Your count is right. So make up your mind. Either you go for help or start climbing."

"I hope you decide to go for help," a voice said behind her. She was so startled she nearly fell into the pool.

"You don't think I'd let you climb alone, again, do you?" her father continued.

"I wasn't seriously considering it," she stammered.

Austin, who was standing behind her father, gave her a knowing wink.

"Let's get this over with," her father grumbled. "We've all got more important things to do."

15

Her cave count corroborated, Nick stood atop the rock dam with Elliot and Austin beside her and explained the ground rules. "Boyle has stashed something here. He left a note in the car to that effect. This cave is part of my Packard, not your Anasazi. So I make the climb with you two here as backup."

"Forget it," Elliot said. "You make a mistake in that chimney and all backup down here is good for is scraping you off the rocks. You climb with a partner."

"You?"

"Take your pick."

"As long as I go first," she said. "And I'm first in the cave. Is that agreed?"

Elliot shrugged as if to say the order of entry was of no importance. But she knew the glint in his eye. She'd seen it often enough in her own mirror.

Lust, or something very like it, at the thought of a major discovery.

Nick pointed up at the smiling mouth. "Look at the size of that cave, Elliot. And the shape. It doesn't fit the Anasazi pattern."

"It's not typical, that's for sure." He nodded at Austin. "What do you think?"

"Considering what we've found so far in this canyon, I don't know what to think. The fact that it's atypical might have made it a perfect hiding place for Anasazi treasures." He stared at Nick. "Or Boyle's."

Elliot grinned. "I think we have a volunteer to go with you."

Nick leaned close to her father, reassessing the glint in his eye. Not lust, she decided, but mischief, maybe even matchmaking. She checked Austin to see if he was in on the conspiracy, but he was studying the chimney and shaking his head. Finally he said, "Let's hope more of that wall doesn't collapse when we're climbing. Otherwise, Elliot's going to need the Corps of Engineers to dig us out."

"One thing's in your favor," Elliot responded. "Whatever's up there ought to be safe enough, because no casual sightseer would risk that chimney."

"Only someone obsessed," Nick replied.

"We should have brought hardhats," Nick said when she'd reached the top of the chimney, the point nearest the cave mouth.

Austin grunted. He'd been pelted by rocks twice on the way up, though none had been large enough to do more than bruise his shoulders and back. Both times, the rock beneath Nick's foot had suddenly crumbled under pressure. And now that she was level with the cave, she realized the opening wasn't as close to the chimney as it appeared from below. To reach it, she'd have to cut holds in the cliff's water-polished face. And in order to do that, she'd have to hang in space, with one foot dangling, the other braced on a heavily fissured sandstone ledge. If that gave way, her life would depend on the rope that attached her to Austin.

She explained her intentions. "Will you be able to hold my weight if you have to?"

Three feet below her, Austin shifted his feet, checking the stability of his position. "Give me a minute." Using the point of his rock hammer, he attacked a crevice near his elbow, shoveling debris onto the canyon floor below, forcing Elliot to cover his head and shout, "Warn me next time!"

Austin dug his hand into the crevice, his biceps bulging as he tested its strength. "I've got a pretty good grip." He didn't sound convinced.

"How the hell did Boyle get up here?" Nick muttered.

"Maybe he didn't."

Which was exactly what she'd been thinking. Certainly, Boyle could have skipped this cave, either because it was too small or too hard to get to, and gone deeper into the canyon for #6. And why not? The numbering system was his alone; it didn't have to be logical.

Nick took a deep breath. "Like you said, every cave has to be checked. Are you ready?"

"As I'll ever be."

Half expecting the worst, she swung her left foot into space and hung there at a crazy angle, waiting for disaster. When nothing happened, she went to work with a small rock hammer and soon had a foothold cut into the sandstone. Once her toe was inserted into it, she righted herself and cut two more holds in the cliff face.

A glance at Austin told her he still looked secure.

"Give me some slack," she said.

His hand left the crevice long enough to play out three feet of rope.

"Another foot," she told him.

He questioned her with a skeptical look but did as she asked. They both knew that if she slipped completely a three-foot fall was enough to dislodge them both, so what did another foot of rope matter?

Tentatively, she raised her boot to the next hole, dug in her toe, and stretched her hand over the lip of the cave. Her fingers felt a notch in the stone. She tested it gingerly. The rock felt solid.

Maybe Boyle had clung to the same notch. No, that didn't make sense. If Boyle had come this way, there should still be evidence of handholds.

"Now," she said without looking at Austin, and raised one leg into the cave.

"More slack."

As soon as she got it, she kicked free of her last foothold and pulled herself inside.

"Thank you, Austin, for coming with me." She collapsed on her back, staring at the etching in the wall beside her. H. BOYLE, 1912 #6. And he'd been here again in 1942, according to the note he'd left for Knute and Nora.

You old bastard. How'd you do it? How'd you make the climb twice on your own? If Elliot hadn't come after her she would have tried to climb alone. Chances were she'd be dead by now.

Boyle must have had help, it was as simple as that. Or he'd been part mountain goat. Or maybe the climb had been easier before the rockfall.

"Are you all right?" Austin shouted.

"I'm fine."

"Well, what do you see?"

"Boyle was here all right. He left his mark."

"And?" he demanded.

"Give me time to look." She dug out her flashlight and played its beam over the walls. No petroglyphs. The cave was shallow, only six feet deep, four feet high, and empty. So much for Boyle's bank.

"You've been robbed," she told his ghost. To Austin, she added, "No sign of the Anasazi."

"Good," he called back. "I wouldn't want to make this trip twice."

I'm still looking, she thought, as she crawled back and forth checking the floor of the cave. Nothing. She played her flashlight over the walls again, moving the beam slowly and cautiously. Even so, she nearly missed it, a narrow fissure in the back wall. Wedged in sideways was a metal box, so corroded it no longer reflected light. It came out with a screech.

The point of her rock hammer sprang the lock. Inside the

lid, Boyle's name was scratched into the metal along with #6. The box was long and narrow, the size of a safe deposit canister. Into it had been crammed a bundle wrapped in oilcloth tied with heavy cord.

"My legs are turning to jelly," Austin shouted.

"Ten minutes."

"I don't have a watch."

"Count, then."

"Your father was right about you!"

Nick ignored him as she settled cross-legged, with the bundle in her lap, her flashlight angled so she could see what she was doing. The twine was badly knotted. Untying it would take too much time.

She was tempted to cut it but decided to wait.

She drank the last of her bottled water. "Dad," she called down, "do you have room for litter in your pack?" At his affirmative she threw the empty plastic bottle down. Another one of Elliot's Rules was "Don't leave litter, ever." She used the room vacated by the bottle to shove the bundle in her backpack. Once it was securely stowed, she checked the cave one more time and crawled out into the sunlight.

"Well?" Austin asked at the sight of her.

"His bank was there as advertised."

"And?"

"In my backpack."

"Dammit!" Elliot called from below. "What's happening?"

"The mother lode!" Nick shouted back, joking. Odds were that she had found nothing more than memorabilia.

"Anasazi?" Elliot asked eagerly.

"No, Baptist Boyle."

1₆

The Ford topped the last rise before
State Highway 24 entered the town of
Green River. From there, U.S. 50
turned east and crossed the river, the
last barrier between Knute and Nora
and their escape into Colorado.

Knute stopped the truck, got out,
and focused his old World War One
binoculars on the town, but it bore no
resemblance to his memories. Instead
of a sleepy rural community, known
only for its watermelons and canta-
loupes, he saw swarms of lawmen man-
ning a roadblock where the two
highways intersected. Beyond the roadblock a stand of cottonwood trees
screened the road from sight.

He handed the binoculars to Nora,
who adjusted them to account for her
nearsightedness.

"They're looking for the Packard,"

she said without taking her eyes from the glasses.

"Sure," he said, trying to sound confident. He slapped the fender of Boyle's dilapidated truck. "They'll never expect us in this flivver."

"Or in these getups," she added.

They eyed one another's disguises from head to foot. Knute wore bib overalls, Nora a housedress that made her look dowdy. Her Thompson was wrapped in a blanket like a baby.

He smiled reassuringly. She answered in kind.

"We're indestructible," Knute said by rote.

"Indestructible," Nora repeated.

Knute opened the passenger door for her and helped her into the passenger's seat.

"Next stop, Colorado," he said, climbing in beside her.

Steam hissed from the radiator as he started the engine. He'd pushed the old car to fifty back on a good stretch of road, and she'd damn near blown a gasket.

"A kiss for luck," he said, leaning toward her.

"For luck." Blinking tears from her eyes, she kissed him.

He gunned the engine and started downhill toward the town.

"Jesus," Knute breathed when they got closer. What looked to be one roadblock from a distance because of the intervening cottonwoods turned out to be a series of barriers crossing the road every twenty yards. Four officers manned each barricade. Turning off the road would land their flivver in the river or hung up in the trees.

Two cops waved them through the first barrier without a second glance. Knute checked the rearview as he eased the Ford toward the second barrier. Behind them, the sawhorses closed as if to block escape. But the cops, in the mirror at least, looked unconcerned, showing no signs they'd recognized Knute and Nora.

When they passed the second barrier just as easily, Nora squeezed his knee and sighed with relief. This time, though, the rearview told a different story. The cops, four to start with, had been reinforced by four more and all eight were suddenly pointing their guns at the back of the flivver.

Ahead of them, the next barrier was fifty yards away and three sawhorses deep. Behind it a phalanx of cops seemed to appear out of nowhere, their rifles and shotguns leveled at the truck.

"They're onto us," Knute whispered.

"I know." Nora touched his knee again, then went to work getting the Thompson ready.

"I love you," he said.

"Me, too. Now go."

Knute floored the old Ford. They were still in first gear when they hit the sawhorses.

Nora's blood splattered on the windshield from a shoulder wound. Knute took a bullet through the thigh.

Cops scattered. Sawhorses splintered as the old Ford smashed through the barrier. For an instant, Knute thought they'd made it only to see a pair of patrol cars pull out of the trees and onto the road directly ahead of them.

Knute jerked the wheel hard over, swinging off the road and heading down the bank toward the Green River. But there were cops there, too, and men in suits, carrying Thompsons just like Nora's.

"What do you think?" Knute shouted over the revving engine. "Do we shoot our way out?"

But her bloody arm hung limp, and the Thompson took two hands.

He handed her his .45. He'd go with the Thompson.

"Ready?" he said as the truck rolled to a stop.

She shook her head. "There's too many of them. We can escape later."

"Knute and Nora together," he answered, "like always."

As one, they stepped out of the Ford, their hands raised high.

A man wearing a dark suit and hat broke cover to stare at them. Around him, more men appeared.

The first man raised an arm and yelled, "Fire."

Knute was reaching for Nora when the bullets struck.

17

Nick rocked on her heels. The first document in the stack was marked TOP SECRET and addressed to Franklin D. Roosevelt. My God! Her joke about the mother lode had come true.

She was in her tent, out of the night wind, with Elliot and Austin watching her unwrap the bundle from the comfort of their camp chairs. They had waited until the two students had gone to their tents for the night.

Dinner had been eaten, rushed through without so much as a memory of taste on Nick's part, before she tackled the oilcloth treasure from cave #6. The cloth, plus an additional lining of wax paper, had preserved the documents perfectly.

Her heart raced. Her fingers tingled as she held up the paper to show off its TOP SECRET stamp.

Before opening the bundle, she'd

spread a plastic tarp on the floor of the tent to protect the contents from grit. She also wore baggies over her hands to safeguard her find.

"It's a short summary of an intelligence report," she said, "signed by Harry H. Woodring, the Secretary of War. 'Pursuant to your request, both naval and army intelligence estimates indicate that the Japanese intend to attack the United States somewhere in the Pacific in the near future, quite probably at Pearl Harbor. At this point in time, however, our agents cannot confirm Pearl Harbor as their target, but it is our best estimate.' "

Nick smiled so hard her chapped lips cracked. "I'd say that's as good as a petroglyph."

Austin snorted. "What you've got there is an interesting historical footnote, nothing more. Although what a man like Boyle was doing with something like this, I can't imagine."

"I don't think these papers belonged to him," Nick replied. "They belonged to someone he knew. A Knute and Nora."

She was startled to see Austin's reaction.

"How do you know that?"

"There was a note, left in the car to a Knute and Nora. It mentioned something about a Green River. Does that ring any bells?"

"The Packard," he exclaimed. "How could I have been so stupid?"

"What about the Packard?" both Scotts yelled.

"That car doesn't belong to Hyrum Boyle, it belongs to a pair of bank robbers. Their names were Knute and Nora and they were almost as famous as Bonnie and Clyde during the Depression. A big, maroon Packard convertible was their trademark. They got killed in the Green River Massacre, but the car was never found."

"There's more," Nick said. "This paper is dated April 23, 1940, more than a year before the Japanese attacked Pearl. And that's not the best part. There's a handwritten notation at the bottom. I quote. 'If need be, we must allow the Japanese to strike the first blow in order to unite the American people for the coming war.' Unquote."

Nick pumped a fist. "The note is initialed FDR."

Elliot whistled.

Austin sputtered, "Wait a minute. That document came out of the Packard, Knute and Nora's car, right?"

"Here's the note I found," Nick answered. "If we believe it, and why shouldn't we, it must have contained loot from the bank. Boyle said he borrowed the money, but kept these papers."

Austin waved aside the note. "Money's one thing, but how the hell did a pair of bank robbers get their hands on a top secret document like that?"

Nick shrugged, but it was a good question, one which she couldn't answer.

Austin continued, "Knute and Nora robbed small, Utah banks only, not federal repositories."

She said, "We know one thing at least. This bundle has been sitting in that cave since 1942, by which time Boyle would have known the importance of the documents."

"Wrong," Austin said. "We don't know when Boyle put it there. We only have his word on paper."

"Why would he go to the trouble of writing out a lie and then climbing up to that cave to stash it?"

Elliot coughed for attention. "You know the rules, Nick. Make no assumptions."

"Fine. Let's see what else we have." She laid the first document aside on the tarp and went on to the next. It, too, was marked TOP SECRET as was the one underneath it. She held one and then the other up for inspection.

"These two deal with Japanese naval and army capabilities as of April 1940, including estimates of aircraft, capital ships, troop strength, and the raw materials they'd stockpiled in case of war. The first is signed by Charles Edison, Secretary of the Navy, the second by Harry Hopkins, Secretary of Commerce, who was also FDR's close personal friend and advisor if I remember my history correctly." She stacked them carefully on top of the first document.

"That still doesn't answer my question," Austin said, shaking his head. "Frankly, I don't buy it, documents like these turning up in the hands of a pair of small-time crooks."

"You said that they were famous for their time," Nick said, a lame response but the best she could manage. She crossed her fingers for luck, hoping the remaining document might hold the answer. She raised its TOP SECRET cover sheet and caught her breath. The words mother lode didn't do this one justice.

"White House stationery," she announced. "Handwritten."

Even the skeptical Austin leaned forward in expectation.

"Fame and fortune," Nick said.

Austin blinked.

"While you two are writing up your petroglyphs for the archaeological journals," Nick explained, "I'll be on the front page of the *New York Times*."

Elliot folded his arms. "All right, daughter, enlighten us."

Nick could barely restrain herself. "It's a note from Roosevelt to Harry Hopkins."

"Signed?" Elliot asked.

"Absolutely."

Elliot rubbed his hands expectantly. "That's better. That, along with the other note, we can authenticate. If the handwriting is Roosevelt's, then Knute and Nora be damned."

"Listen to this," Nick said. " 'Dear Harry, I've been thinking over our discussion. I'm now convinced that it may be necessary to provoke the Japanese into attacking us. I see no other way of turning the tide of isolationism. I take comfort, however, from the fact that war is, I believe, inevitable. Yours, Franklin.' "

Austin reached for the letter.

"Baggies, first," Nick told him.

Dutifully, Austin encased his hands in plastic. "Jesus, look at the date. If this is real, it means an American president deliberately allowed American servicemen to be killed."

"It gets worse," she said. "If memory serves, we moved our Pacific fleet from San Diego to Pearl in early 1941. Had it stayed where it was, the Japanese might not have attacked. Maybe that's what Roosevelt meant in the note. Maybe he moved the fleet as a deliberate provocation."

"Or to be sacrificed," Austin added.

"Hold it," Elliot said. "Rule number one."

"I remember," Nick answered. "Never take anything on face value, verify first. You see, Elliot, I was listening in class."

Austin handed the letter on to a properly baggied Elliot, who read to himself before saying, "It looks real to me, so we

82

might as well give in, Austin. From now on, my daughter's going to be hogging the limelight. Her fifteen minutes of fame is just around the corner."

"They could be forgeries," Austin pointed out.

Elliot shook his head. "Why forge documents you aren't going to use and then hide them away? Besides, sixty years ago most Americans didn't know where Pearl Harbor was, so they sure as hell wouldn't expect the Japanese to bomb it."

"I've got you there," Nick said. "In 1924, General Billy Mitchell predicted that the Japanese would bomb Pearl Harbor from the air. His foresight got him demoted and court-martialed. And then there's the rumors, urban myths if you like, that Roosevelt knew all along the Japanese were going to attack and that he turned a blind eye in order to draw America into the war. Look at lend-lease. It was his way of coming to Churchill's aid and still remaining neutral. Until now, that is. And now, these documents change history."

Austin said, "Billy Mitchell, I remember but . . ."

Elliot nudged Austin with an elbow. "You're wasting your time. She wins at Trivial Pursuit, too."

Refusing to be sidetracked, Nick moved on to the three remaining documents in the bundle. All were handwritten; all agreed with Roosevelt's assessment of the situation in the Pacific; and all of them endorsed Roosevelt's proposed remedy of the situation, an early entry in the war so that England wouldn't have to stand alone. The letters were signed by Jerold Thomas, Dana Koplin, and Gordon Hanover, names none of them recognized.

"You've got a lot of work ahead of you," Elliot said. "You'll have to authenticate everything, names and all."

"Once I do, there's going to be a feeding frenzy in the media. It's our new national pastime, destroying reputations."

"That's why I stick to the long dead," Elliot said. "They're safer. They don't have any relatives left alive to sue you."

"Are you advising me to sit on these documents?"

"I'm asking you to put World War Two on hold until we finish with Boyle's Twist. Austin and I want to move on to the next cave."

"Number four! You saw it yourself. It's a bastard."

"It's next in line."

"Name me another Anasazi site with a climb like that."

Elliot pursed his lips. "You're right about that. On the other hand, a climb like that would have discouraged the Anasazi's enemies. It also might have been chosen as a hiding place for something very important."

"Certainly, we can't pass it by," Austin said.

"Are you offering to volunteer to go first?" Nick asked.

Austin's Adam's apple bobbed at the suggestion. "You're our best climber."

"Who says?"

"After today, I do."

Nick turned to her father. "And you, Elliot?"

He shrugged. "I taught you, so what do you expect?"

She shook her head. "The Anasazi have been waiting in this canyon for a thousand years. They can wait one more day while I tend to Pearl Harbor."

18

Irma Slater, wearing her best black dress and Sunday shoes, slowly climbed the narrow stairs to Decker's Detective Agency. The advertisement in the phone book—"We specialize in divorce cases"—hadn't deterred her. It was the only detective agency listed in the Provo directory. To make matters worse, it was situated in a rundown two-story frame building on Ninth South, not the best part of town even without the beer hall downstairs.

Her dress, made over from a hand-me-down from her church, hung loosely on her bony frame. Her shoes, shined that morning, had half-inch heels that made her back ache with a vengeance. These days it ached constantly anyway, a reminder of her sins and the extra houses she had to clean to be able to afford a detective. The pain was also God's way of punishing

Irma for the way she'd brought up her daughter.

The landing at the top of the stairs was no bigger than a throw rug. Irma, who'd been tiptoeing the last few steps, hesitated in front of the door. Fancy black letters on its frosted glass panel read LAMAR DECKER, PROP. From inside came the sound of hunt-and-peck typing.

A sudden chill made her shiver. God's warning, maybe, or the devil's touch. *Let well enough alone*, her minister had said. *Your daughter has paid for her crimes, now let her rest.*

Irma hunched her shoulders against the cold inside her. "Decker," she mouthed. What kind of name was that? What kind of man would do such work, spying on people for divorces?

The kind she needed, Irma told herself. Besides, there was no one else. The police had treated her like a criminal, as if she were no better than her daughter, Nora.

Let's pray for her, the minister had said, but the look in his eyes said he knew Nora was burning in hell.

Irma straightened her shoulders. Hell or not, Nora deserved justice at least and there was no one else to see to her. Irma's husband was long dead and there wasn't so much as a cousin close enough to call kin for a hundred miles.

She touched the doorknob half-expecting it to burn her hand. When it didn't, she grabbed hold and opened the door onto a room just big enough for a wooden teacher's desk with two straight-backed, ladder chairs facing it. Behind the desk, two fingers poised over a typewriter, sat a man not much older than Nora. His smile was as slick as the one Knute wore when he wormed into Nora's good graces. Irma steeled herself to deal with such a person.

Lamar Decker took one look at the woman in the doorway and saw his own poverty-stricken mother, God rest her soul. Guilt made him smile.

"I'm Nora Slater's mother," the woman announced. "Irma Slater."

"As in Knute and Nora?"

"That's right, young man." She tucked hair into the bun at the back of her head, another gesture that evoked the image of his mother.

He said, "Please sit down."

"The police murdered my baby," she continued the moment she was seated primly. "So this Christmas I promised myself I'd do something about it."

She opened her purse and spread ten one-dollar bills on his desk. "I'm a washerwoman. I've been saving nickels and dimes ever since my Nora was shot."

Her tone, like his mother's, set his teeth on edge. He resisted the temptation to look over his shoulder to see if his mother's spirit had materialized to haunt him.

He unclenched his teeth to say, "What do you expect for ten dollars?" Even as he spoke, he knew she couldn't spare it, that it was probably all she had.

"I read in the paper that one of the state troopers said my baby and her man were trying to surrender when they got shot." She shook her head. "That doesn't sound fair. That's why I want you to find out the truth."

"There's a war on, don't you know?"

"That's not my concern, young man. All I want is justice for my baby."

Decker sighed. He remembered reading about Knute and Nora's final shoot-out. At the time, he hadn't given it a second thought. They'd gone on a murder spree and gotten what they deserved. That's what the papers said anyway, not that he believed any of the crap they printed. And he ought to know, what with the fiction he produced in divorce court, duly reported of course by the news hawks.

"Always before, the newspapers loved my daughter," the woman went on. "They printed as many pictures of her as they did the president. I've got a scrapbook at home to prove it."

"I'm sure you do."

"Just hear me out, young man." She glared at him, waiting for him to respond.

"Yes, ma'am."

She nodded, satisfied, and continued. "My neighbors used to say, 'You should be proud of your daughter. She's doing what the rest of us don't have the nerve to do. Take money away from those damn banks who are always foreclosing on folks like us.' "

True enough, he thought, remembering the stories from the Depression.

" 'I'd never shoot anybody unless they tried to shoot me first,' that's what my Nora told me. The papers printed those same words, so you know I'm not lying. A Christian mother wouldn't do that."

He winced at the echo of his own psalm-singing mother. *Help out the poor old lady*, she was saying. *Do it for my memory*.

Decker winced. Knute and Nora were cop killers. Which meant the cops would be all over him if he started asking questions. They might even lift his license.

He shook his head. "I'm afraid ten dollars won't go very far, Mrs. Slater."

"Then do what you can."

He leaned across the desk and pushed the money back at her. "Please, you keep it."

She stood up, smoothing her threadbare dress and fussing with her bun. "A deal is a deal, young man. You ought to know that."

"It's been over a year since the shoot-out. Memories fade."

"No, people don't forget a thing like that. I don't have a phone, so you'll have to wait for me to be in touch. I'm depending on you."

"Mrs. Slater," he began but he was speaking to a closing door.

He stared at the money. The wrinkled bills looked as if they'd been wadded into balls, then smoothed out for the occasion. Probably she hid them under her mattress just as his mother had done.

"Okay," he said out loud for his mother's benefit, "I'll make a couple of calls. But the cops are going to kill me."

19

Nick loaded the documents into the satchel and carried them to one of their two Jeeps. As always in the desert, she raised the Cherokee's hood and visually inspected the oil, the radiator coolant, brake fluid, and even the level in the reservoir that held the windshield cleaner. Once that was done, she inspected the lever-action .30-.30 she kept under the front seat. She'd already stowed five gallons of bottled water in the back.

The map legend for this area of Utah bore a highlighted warning: CARRY DRINKING WATER IN THIS AREA. The warning ran alongside the road to Baptist Wash.

Once underway, Nick decided the map was wrong. What it showed as a road was actually a pair of car-width ruts that limited her speed to fifteen miles an hour. Even then, the tires kicked up a red rooster tail of dust. The temperature was in the high 90s so she ran with the windows open rather than risk a boil-over with the air conditioner. The air smelled vaguely of creosote.

By the time she turned onto State Highway 95 an hour later, Nick was caked with dust. Her mouth felt gritty and her eyes burned from squinting against the sunlight, despite dark glasses and the pulled-down visor of her Cubs cap.

With asphalt under her, she switched on the air conditioner and made the twenty miles to Hanksville, the nearest town, in fifteen minutes.

To call Hanksville a town was stretching the point, Nick decided as she parked in front of the Redrock Café and General Store. Her Utah guide, which she'd used to acquaint herself with the area prior to joining her father's dig, had described Hanksville as a boomtown with a growing population of four hundred. It was the hub of highways, or so said the guide, standing on the bank of the Dirty Devil River. Originally, its desolate location had attracted Ebenezer Hanks, a polygamist fleeing from the law, as well as Butch Cassidy's Wild Bunch.

The Redrock Café, a single-story clapboard with a two-story front, looked as if it had last been painted in Butch's day. Its dilapidated wooden siding was covered with signs. GAS. GRO-CERIES. MOTEL. EXPLOSIVES. COCA-COLA. SQUIRT. BEER. POST OFFICE.

A brick house had been built against one side wall as if to shore up the entire structure. Nick guessed both dated from the early 1900s.

Before she could move, the café's screen door banged and a short, dark-haired woman stepped out onto the wooden side-walk. She shaded her eyes with one hand while beckoning Nick inside with the other.

Nick climbed out of the Jeep, slapping dust from her clothes.

"Don't worry about that," the woman said. "Around here you get used to it. Come on in. You look like you could use a cold drink."

Inside, the woman opened the lid on an old-fashioned cooler and fished out a can of Coke, dripping cold water.

"Coke's all we've got, I'm afraid, until the next delivery truck."

Nick held the icy can against her forehead.

The woman said, "My name's Joan Nay. If I had to guess, I'd say you're one of the archaeologists rooting around out there at the Devil's Door. Nick Scott, isn't it?"

Nick blinked.

"Don't look so surprised. Your party put up at the Poor Boy Motel down the street when you arrived last week."

"We arrived in the dark," Nick said, "and left at dawn."

Nay smiled. "We don't get many tourists here, especially this time of year. And folks like you, archaeologists, are a real treat. For a day or two you rivaled satellite TV. And no, no one spied on you in case you're wondering. You have a couple of students with you, don't you?"

When Nick nodded, Nay continued. "Since we're the only place in town open at night where else could they buy a beer and brag about their work? Now, what can I do for you?"

"I'd hoped the post office might have a copy machine."

"Heavens, all we've got is a few mailing envelopes, stamps and a postage scale. But I've got a copier next door you're welcome to use."

"Only if I can pay." Procedure called for a working copy of her documents, plus at least one backup. "Would a quarter a copy be all right?"

The woman laughed. "Those are big city prices. What kind of a person would I be if I charged you that much? Ten cents will do. Give me the things you want copied and I'll do it for you."

Nick hesitated. "These are historical documents."

"Historical documents? You must have found some of old man Boyle's notes, I'll bet. He was always writing down things about those Indians he was so crazy about."

"Did you know him?"

"By sight mostly. He wasn't much of a talker. At one time my father was a drinking buddy of his, on those rare times when Boyle got into town."

"What did your father think of him?" Nick asked.

Nay stared at some point beyond Nick as if to bring the past into sharper focus. "I remember him saying once that Boyle was the craziest friend he'd ever had. Boyle called himself a cave man."

"Do you know what he meant by that?"

"He liked to live in them, I guess. Which proves he was crazy if you've seen those caves in the Twist."

"That's where my father's working right now."

"That's fathers for you," Nay said with a wink. "Mine went climbing with Boyle once. After that, he wouldn't set foot in the Twist. He said it was crazy to climb those walls. Boyle went up and down, my father said, like a monkey. It was a fall that finally did him in, you know. He fell and broke half the bones in his body. He was dead by the time they found him. It was the way he would have wanted to go, my father said at the time, doing what he wanted." Nay grinned. "Me, I always wanted to be tall, skinny, and redheaded, and look what happened. Short and brown haired. Now let's get those copies made. I live right next door."

Seen from a distance, the house alongside the general store was as dull and lifeless as its coarse brick walls. But up close, light sparkled from its gables where chunks of colored glass had been set into the stucco under the eaves.

"My father was a bottle collector," Nay said as she paused to point out the glitter. "He was at it for years, until he filled the entire garage. That's when my mother put her foot down and told him to get rid of the mess. So he smashed the best ones and plastered in the pieces."

She sighed at the memory. "I was always partial to the blue medicine bottles myself."

Inside, the living room had high ceilings, elaborate wain-scoting, and marbleized linoleum on the floors. Flowered paper covered the walls. Old-fashioned roll-up blinds had been drawn against the desert heat.

A breakfast nook off the kitchen had been turned into an office, complete with a computer, copier, and fax.

Nick had made only one set of copies of the documents when the machine jammed.

"It does that quite a lot these days," the woman said. "It's really a very old model." She opened the machine up and extracted some crumpled pieces of paper. "Let's try that again, shall we?"

The next copy came out totally black.

"Oh dear, I was afraid of that. It looks like the drum is gone. I really should have called the repair man last week. If I call him now, he'll be here by tomorrow morning. I don't know if you'd like to wait. Or if you trust me, you can just leave your papers here and pick up the copies tomorrow afternoon."

Nick took the one copy from her before sealing the originals in the heavy plastic bags she always carried for the protection of artifacts. Then she eyed the fax. It tempted her. With it, she could transmit copies of her find to the Smithsonian for verification. But to whom? She hadn't worked there long enough to make any close friends and the director, who'd hired her, had also fired her. True, he was a friend of Elliot's, but not friend enough to stand against the political pressure Nick had generated on her Alaskan dig. It wasn't her fault that people had gotten killed. "You made a mistake," Elliot told her at the time. "You told them the truth about what happened."

So forget the fax and do your own research. That way nobody beats you to publication, she thought to herself.

Elliot was expecting her back tonight. She inwardly groaned at the thought of making the trip again, but it would have to be done. She already had one copy. She would take that with her. She made a decision. Joan Nay looked like a woman who could be trusted.

"I'd like to borrow your computer," Nick told the woman, "and do some research on the Net."

"Of course. While you do that, I'll fix us some Mormon tea."

Nick logged onto the Smithsonian site, crossed her fingers, and entered her password. A moment later she was in, her luck holding. No one had gotten around to deleting her from the system.

Then she hesitated. The Smithsonian site recorded all logons. She mentally kicked herself. What was she worrying about? She was in Hanksville, Utah, for God's sake, the middle of nowhere.

She began by entering the names from the documents that were unknown to her, Jerold Thomas, Dana Koplin, and Gordon Hanover.

Thomas and Koplin had both been advisors to Roosevelt; both FDR's classmates at Harvard. And both had died in 1941. Not exactly confirmation of her find, but at least those two had been alive when the documents were written.

She tried cross-referencing them with Knute and Nora Deacons but came up empty.

The Smithsonian's database had no record of Gordon Hanover.

Nick was about to probe further when the Smithsonian site dumped her. Rather than waste time reconnecting, she drank her Mormon tea—hot water, cream, and sugar—and then went back to the post office to mail her copy of the documents to her father's address in Albuquerque, which was where she was living for the time being. But only until she had a permanent job, she reminded herself. Until then, though, there was no getting around the fact that she was back to living at home like an undergraduate.

Robb Neff, an archivist at the FBI
headquarters building on Pennsylvania
Avenue, groaned in frustration as his
computer froze. He resisted the temptation to pound his fist on the keyboard
and settled for a one-fingered tap on
the escape key. Nothing. Well, that's
what you got for buying software from
the lowest bidder.

He checked the clock. The assistant
director wanted Neff's project on his
desk before the end of the day. If his
system was about to crash, that deadline would be out the window and Neff
would find himself working an all-
nighter.

The computer's screen went blank.

"Please," he murmured, praying to
the gods of binary information.

The computer beeped and there it

was, deep shit, in the form of a single word, WAITING.

Only twice before had that happened. Both times, thank God, it had been a test of the internal security system. Even so, there'd been hell to pay because of procedural errors, one of them his. His only penance had been a written explanation, since he was relatively new to the bureau. He was two years out of Stanford Engineering School and on the fast track to success, or so he'd been told, because of his computer expertise. He'd taken the job, as a civil service shelter rather than face the hypertension of Silicon Valley.

But if this wasn't a test. Just the thought started him breathing hard. He crossed his fingers and started counting the passing seconds to himself. At ten he began to breathe easier.

Maybe the server was stacked up, maybe WAITING meant nothing more ominous. Merely a signal to wait his turn in the data queue.

A high-pitched beep, repetitive and gut-wrenching, sounded. An instant later THIS IS NOT A TEST appeared on his computer. An alert was coming through.

He entered his acceptance code.

The onscreen response told him that the FBI's security scanning system had detected three red-flagged names at play on the Internet. Two might be coincidence, but three had to be checked, particularly when used in tandem.

Neff checked the offending site, the Smithsonian. Next, he verified the origination point, Hanksville, Utah. He blinked in disbelief at the sight of it. He'd never heard of Hanksville. He reverified. Sure enough, Hanksville it was.

His arms trembled as if he'd been overworking weights at the gym.

Relax, he told himself. His red-flag briefing had said most system hits were false alarms. Usually researchers or history buffs were to blame. But protocol still had to be followed. And protocol told him to buck the alert up the chain of command to his deputy director, Miles Craycroft.

Craycroft glared at the file he'd been handed.

"It's protocol, sir," Neff said. "A red-flag alert."

"I'm aware of that."

"It's not a test, sir. I checked."

"Thank you."

Craycroft continued glaring until Neff had backed out of the office and closed the door behind him.

Christ almighty, Craycroft mouthed silently, knowing full well that the building had more bugs than a slum did cockroaches. He took a deep breath. The secret to success was remaining calm and making no sudden moves. Or sudden decisions, either. Both created waves in what, experience had taught him, was a world of red tape. And often as not the tape was attached to a piece of shit like one of those chocolate Hershey kisses with a tassel.

He sat down and placed the protocol file on his spotless desk pad. He centered it carefully, then tapped a manicured finger on the CONFIDENTIAL cover sheet. These days damn near everything started out being classified CONFIDENTIAL, then got bumped up to SECRET at the slightest whim. TOP SECRET was when the boat started to rock.

Craycroft smoothed his thinning hair. Total baldness, he figured, was no more than a crisis away. Under stress, he shed like a sheepdog.

He eyeballed his calendar. Today's agenda included golf with the director after work. That is, if the waves didn't drown him first.

Craycroft sucked a quick breath and turned back the cover sheet. The names hit him like a fist. He knew them by heart; he'd been forced to memorize them when he took the job. Use of the three together, depending on circumstances, could activate the Spider File, for which he was the designated guardian. It was a file that went all the way back to J. Edgar Hoover himself. It hadn't been active in years.

"And God help anyone who activates it," his predecessor had warned him during the transition briefing. That had been five years ago. During that time Craycroft had never set eyes on the file, but he and he alone, except for the director, had the combination to the humidity-controlled safe where it was kept. A safe not ten feet from where he sat. A safe in plain sight, sunk deeply into a reinforced concrete wall. Bomb- and fire-proof. Even where he sat, Craycroft could feel the vibration of hidden machinery that provided the safe's constant climate control.

"Would I be the one to activate it in case of emergency?" Craycroft had asked at the end of his briefing.

"Don't ask me," his predecessor had said. "It never came up in my time. If it does in yours—and pray God it doesn't—your job is to follow the instructions in the file."

At the memory of their conversation, saliva filled Craycroft's mouth. His attempted swallow, sharp edged and painful, backfired and started him choking.

By the time the fit passed, he was praying that Neff was merely being an alarmist. But when he read further, he saw that Neff had verified the alert, following procedure.

In his mind's eye, Craycroft saw a tidal wave building. Someone in Utah was researching the names. And Utah was a trigger factor. He remembered that from his briefing.

On wobbly legs, he approached the safe. His equally unsteady fingers botched the first try at dialing the combination. He knelt, bringing the dial to eye level. He drew one deep breath, then another. His fingers calmed enough to input the proper numbers.

The door opened. The safe, deep enough to hold Craycroft's entire desk, contained only a thick, sealed folder and a smaller, letter-sized unsealed envelope with Craycroft's name on it.

Craycroft stayed where he was, on his knees, as he read the letter inside the unsealed envelope. It was addressed to him and dated January 2, 2001. Christ, that was only six months ago. Which meant the director himself had to have updated it.

The letter was only a single paragraph long.

The sealed envelope in this safe may be opened only by the Director himself or by Ms. Beverly Zeien, Special Counsel to the Department of Justice. Once you've passed it on, Mr. Craycroft, your job is over. Knowledge of this file is classified Q. Revelation of its existence will be considered an act of treason.

Craycroft locked the safe, rose on legs that felt artificial, and shuffled back to his desk. By now the director would be on his way to their golf date. Meeting him on the course with the Spider File in hand was impossible. Besides, the director was relatively new, the latest political appointee. A man like that would want to preserve his deniability in the event the shit hit the fan.

A Q clearance could mean anything, including national security.

Breathing hard, Craycroft checked the in-house phone directory, in itself a classified document. Zeien's number was not an internal extension but a number in Virginia.

Craycroft was sweating down to his fingertips as he punched in the area code on his secure line.

2₁

Nick was exhausted. The setting sun had shone in her eyes for the entire return trip to the campsite. She reached the escarpment that formed the base of the slot canyons and stopped. Something was wrong. There was no sign of the other Jeep. In fact, there was no sign of anything.

She felt her shoulders slump. Had she gotten herself lost? Maybe taken a wrong turnoff? She switched off the motor and stepped out of the Jeep. There, in the distance, stood Baptist Boyle's boulder. This had to be the right place.

"Elliot, Austin!" she called out, but there was nothing but silence. The light was fading and making it more difficult for her tired eyes to pick out landmarks.

She grabbed her cell phone and dialed Elliot's number, but got no answer. Dammit, Elliot, this was no time to switch off. She tried his number again. Still no answer.

"Don't panic," she told herself. It would be better to wait for the morning and retrace her steps. There had to be more than one huge volcanic boulder in the area. Sure, Elliot would be frantic, but it couldn't be helped. She resigned herself to an uncomfortable night in the Jeep.

The morning light did nothing but increase her confusion. Except for the absence of any signs of habitation she could swear she was practically sitting on top of the campsite. There was the entrance to Burro Gulch and over to the right Boyle's Twist. She rubbed her eyes. They felt gritty, thanks to a restless night in the Jeep.

She stifled a yawn and checked her water. She definitely had enough for a full day. She grabbed her rifle and headed for the volcanic rock where Baptist Boyle's shack had once stood.

Early as it was, the heat was already uncomfortable enough to start her sweating after a few steps. After a few yards she felt like she was hallucinating. There was no Packard. And instead of her carefully preserved excavation of Boyle's "garage," there was nothing there but a shallow depression filled with rubble.

"Dammit!" she cried. What the hell was happening?

She levered a round into her .30-.30. Elliot's Rule: Examine the facts. Okay, what were the facts? She was here on a site that looked remarkably like one that she had been excavating two days before. Hell, it had to be the same site. But her precious Packard was gone. There was no sign of the metal panels or wooden doors that had formed the entrance to the garage. And where were Elliot and the others?

"Either you're disoriented," she told herself, "or something happened to them."

Chances were that the area was littered with volcanic rocks similar to the one she had taken as a marker. There was only one way to make sure.

Nick racked her brain trying to remember which cave was the easiest climb and headed for what she thought of as Boyle's Twist. Boyle's site number three came to mind, an uninteresting cave but an easy climb.

"I guess easiest is relative," she gasped as she finally struggled over the ledge of the entrance. She'd left her climbing equipment at the camp which apparently had vanished into thin air. Without equipment, the "easy" climb had taken hours and resulted in a badly scraped knee and several bloodied fingers.

The cave was shallow and low. Nick slid along the edge and examined the entrance. His mark was there, just like all the others. This was Boyle's Twist.

"Hyrum," she said out loud. "I was never so glad to see your graffiti in all my life." She traced the inscription, Boyle #3, with her fingers. "Now, I know that I'm not lost."

No, she thought to herself. You're not lost, but everybody else is. A rising tide of adrenaline filled her with a mixture of rage and fear. Just what the hell was going on?

22

Night was falling by the time Nick stopped at Joan Nay's. A light shone through the multicolored bottles as Nick knocked on the door. No one answered her knock.

"Joan," Nick called out. "I need to talk to you. It's important."

"Go away," a timid voice answered. "I've already gone to bed."

Nick pounded hard on the door. "I'm not going away until you open up." She continued to bang.

The door was opened abruptly. "For heaven's sake, go away," Nay said.

"Joan, I have to get those documents back that I left with you."

"I don't know what you are talking about. I've never seen you in my life."

"What are you talking about? I sat in your kitchen day before yesterday. Your copier broke down so I left my documents with you."

"Miss, you're as crazy as Groggin's goat. I don't have a copier. Now go away."

"I'm not crazy," Nick shouted, but almost felt as if she were. "You have a copier in your breakfast nook."

She pushed the door open and strode into the kitchen. The breakfast nook was filled with a chrome dinette set. There was no equipment.

"Are you satisfied?" Nay asked. "Now you get out of here before I call the police. I'm a law-abiding person and I don't want trouble. I've never seen you before in my life and I didn't copy any documents and you didn't mail any either."

Nick could see that the woman was nearly in tears. She was lying, but Nick felt that she was trying to tell her something.

"You really have to leave," the Nay woman continued.

"I'm sorry," Nick said and wasn't sure why she was apologizing. She left the house and heard the bolt lock behind her.

She suddenly realized how tired she was. I've got to get some sleep, she thought. I'll work out a plan of action in the morning.

Nick ignored the NO VACANCY sign outside the Poor Boy Motel and went in to see for herself. The clerk recognized her from her previous visit.

"Wouldn't you know it," he said, "we don't get any takers for weeks and suddenly we're as busy as Green River. If you're looking for a room you're out of luck."

"I just need a cot, anything. I'll sleep in the lobby, if you'll let me."

"No can do. The archaeologists have checked in."

"Thank God," Nick said. A surge of relief swept over her. "What rooms are they in?"

"You can talk to one of them right over there, miss." The clerk pointed to a sandy-haired man walking away at the other end of the lobby.

"Austin," Nick called out, but the man didn't stop.

Nick ran to catch up with him and touched him on the shoulder. At her touch, he turned. The man wasn't Reed Austin. He had Austin's coloring and general build, but the resemblance ended there.

"I'm sorry," Nick managed to stammer. "I thought you were an archaeologist."

"So does my wife, my dear, and occasionally even some of my students. Dr. Jon Woodruff at your service." He gave her a courtly bow.

"I'm terribly sorry, I mistook you for Dr. Reed Austin. The man at the desk told me that archaeologists had checked in here."

"And so we have. I've heard of Dr. Austin although we do not share the same campus. I am the leader of a small party from BYU." After a moment he clarified, "That's Brigham Young University from up in Provo. And you are . . . ?"

Nick felt a hot blush of embarrassment. She held out her hand. "I'm Dr. Nicolette Scott. I was hoping to met Dr. Austin and my father here."

"Dr. Elliot Scott? My dear, what a pleasure." He took both her hands in his. "Please assure your father that as far as I'm concerned the Anasazi are his exclusive province. His watershed work on the Anasazi Empire assures that. No one else in the field comes close."

"Why are you here," Nick asked, "if not for the Anasazi?"

"The *Book of Mormon* tells us that American Indians are direct descendants of the lost tribes of Israel." Woodruff smiled to let her know that he knew she was a nonbeliever. "Your father's work has dated the Anasazi as far back as eight hundred B.C. But what if they go back all the way to the migration from Israel? One day, we're hoping to prove just that." He smiled shyly. "Is there any chance of meeting the great man?"

"As soon as we connect I'm certain he'd enjoy talking to you," she answered politely. "However, we seem to have missed each other."

"I had no idea he was in the area. You've not started your dig, have you?"

Nick hesitated. She decided not to mention Boyle's Twist. "Not yet. We're on our way south."

"Let me know if I can be of any assistance." Just then a group of young people crowded into the office. "Plenty of strong backs here, you see."

He waved good-bye as he was swept away by a surge of eager students, no doubt bent on finding something to eat. She returned to the motel clerk.

"Is there anyplace else in town where I can find a place to stay?" she asked.

"This time of night, people don't like taking in strangers," the clerk said. "You could try driving east to Green River, but if I was you I'd head north. Torrey's an easy drive even in the dark. After Torrey you've got Bicknell and Sigurd. There are a couple of decent motels there. Shoot, there's a string of towns all the way to Salt Lake. You might even find a Best Western somewhere. Gentiles have been thick as flies around here since last night, buzzing around and asking all sorts of questions."

"Gentiles?" Nick asked, thoroughly confused, then remembered that Mormons thought of all nonbelievers as Gentiles. "What did they want?"

"You being a Gentile, yourself, you probably don't know what I properly mean." He lowered his voice and whispered conspiratorially. "Men in black, you know? With their shiny sunglasses and their knowing ways. Who knows what they were really after. They certainly don't confide in the natives. Besides what could we tell them. Nothing interesting happens around here." He sounded sorry he hadn't been able to oblige.

"You should have made up something. It would have given them something to do."

He grinned and hunched his shoulders. "Around here, people haven't thought much of Gentiles since the army invaded."

She looked to see if he was joking but saw no sign of it. The invasion he was talking about took place in 1857, when troops of the federal government stormed Utah to put an end to polygamy. The troops had been forced to back off when Brigham Young threatened to burn Salt Lake City to the ground.

"I'll tell you one thing. Those gentlemen were sure making a fuss over at the post office. Don't know how Sister Nay put up with it. Only good thing that came out of it is that the post office has a bright new copying machine. Never did see the likes of it before. As my Daddy used to say, 'Beware of Gentiles bearing gifts.' " He laughed at his joke, unaware that Nick had gone pale.

She bit her lip. "Thanks for the information. I'd better get moving, if I'm going to find a place." Her fatigue evaporated. She was determined to drive all night. She felt like Alice down the rabbit hole, but she was determined to catch the rabbit.

23

Lamar Decker had moved his one-man detective agency to Salt Lake in 1943, hoping to cash in on the divorce boom during the war. He'd collaborated, with the help of a lawyer he'd known, on many a Dear-John letter, money being no object to lonely wives striking it rich in defense work.

But the boom had run out when the ammunition factories closed down, and Decker, who hadn't saved a dime, had been forced to work out of his apartment, a room and half-bath over the Broadway Café on Third South. His desk, fronted by a single client's chair, faced the door in a businesslike manner, but there was no hiding the fact that he slept there, too. Even folded and tucked against the wall, his cot stuck out like a sore thumb.

The knock startled him. He hadn't had a walk-in in months. He opened the door cautiously, expecting his landlord demanding his unpaid rent.

"This place smells," Irma Slater complained the moment she crossed the threshold.

"It's the café downstairs," he apologized. "It's Monday, corn beef and cabbage day."

"If you say so."

"How can I help you?"

"You've got a bad memory, young man. Five years ago I paid you good money to find out who murdered my daughter and her husband."

"Christ!"

"That's a bad habit, taking the Lord's name in vain. If my Nora had said such a thing I would have washed her mouth out with soap."

"I remember now. Irma Slater." He also remembered the ten dollars she'd paid, expecting miracles. "I did the best I could. I sent you a report."

"I'm no fool, young man. In this life, you get what you pay for." She swept past him and took a seat in front of his desk, tapping her foot impatiently until he moved around to sit facing her.

The last time he'd seen Irma Slater she'd been wearing loose hand-me-downs and a dispirited look that reminded him of his mother. That same look, etched even more deeply, was still there on her face. But this time her clothes looked new, off-the-rack at JCPenney's if he was any judge. Sharp-edged wrinkles made him suspect they'd never been worn before.

Decker squirmed. He had twelve dollars in his wallet, with only a couple of cheap divorces pending. Any day now he'd be evicted and forced to live out of his car.

Irma snapped open her purse and fished out a wad of bills, the same as she'd done at his Provo office. Only then she'd counted out ones. Now she was counting out hundred-dollar bills. His jaw fell.

"I went to the Coast and got myself a job in a war plant," she told him as she laid out number ten. "Now I can afford real justice for my baby, my Nora."

Behind her glasses, her red-rimmed, accusing eyes stared at

him the same way his mother's eyes had done. Irma could have been her sister. His mother had worked herself to death, putting him through one year of college, for all the good it had done him.

To escape her eyes, Decker focused on the hundred-dollar bills spread across his desk. A thousand dollars would turn his life around. His eyes watered.

"I hit a dead-end last time," he reminded her, feeding his conscience. "That state trooper changed his story. He said your daughter shot first."

She shook her head. "A reporter wrote it down and put it in the newspaper. So it must be true."

He tore his eyes from the money. "People get misquoted all the time."

"I've kept the clipping." She dug into her purse and came up with a celluloid pocket. She carefully extracted a faded piece of newsprint and spread it on the desk beside the money. "It says here, 'It looked to me like Knute and Nora were trying to surrender when the shooting started.' " She'd quoted from memory, never taking her eyes off Decker.

He grabbed hold of his knees and held on tight to keep from reaching for the cash. For years he'd taken money from his mother without realizing that earning it was killing her.

"Sometimes newspapers get things wrong because they're in such a hurry to get out the news," he said. "That state trooper told me they misquoted him."

"Did you talk to him in person? Did you look him in the eye?"

Decker wet his lips, remembering that he'd tracked the man down by phone.

Irma nodded as if reading his mind. Women had the gift all right, to make you feel guilty no matter what.

"I want you to talk to the others who were there when my Nora was murdered. I want to know what really happened. I'd do it myself, but people don't pay any attention to a woman like me."

If he closed his eyes, that could be his mother talking.

"It's a waste of money," he said. "Too many years have gone by. Memories will have faded."

"You don't forget people being shot to death." Her head turned from side to side as she took in his room. "It don't look to me that you can be so choosy, Mr. Decker, not if I'm willing to spend my hard-earned money."

My hard-earned money had been one of his mother's dirges, one he hadn't appreciated until it was too late.

"I've got divorces waiting," he said. His own included. "Besides, tracking people down after all this time could take forever. My advice is to put your money in the bank."

"Like you say, it's my money, and I don't care how much it costs or how long it takes."

"The war plants are closed," he reminded her. "There's no longer a shortage of men to fill the good jobs."

"I know what you're saying, Mr. Decker, that I won't be able to earn anymore unless I go back to scrubbing floors. That's fine by me if you can help my Nora."

He'd been reading the want-ads long enough to know cops were making a hundred and a quarter a week, a cook half that. A shamus ought to be worth somewhere in between.

He took a single bill. "I'll see what I can do. Come back in a week."

If you can't help her you'll have to give that money back, his mother said from the grave.

24

Nick drove up to the archaeology building at the University of Utah situated in the foothills above Salt Lake City. Even in her exhaustion, she marveled at the lush green surroundings of the campus. She remembered Austin telling her that it was a land-grant college and much of the campus was on the former site of Fort Douglas, an old army post. She parked the Jeep illegally and hurried up the hill toward the building. A flood of students poured out as somewhere a clock tolled the hour.

Nick was too tired to force her way through the crowd. She stood still while the chatting, boisterous young people surged past. The crowd was thinning when Art Clawson practically walked into her. A look of horror spread over his face and he dropped his books. Before Nick could say a word, he started to run.

"I'm getting too old for this," she muttered to herself as she took off after him. She was lucky because they were heading down the hill. Clawson had never been much help on the dig and he wasn't a good runner. A life of all-night study sessions apparently had debilitated him. But Nick was tired and if he hadn't taken a header she might not have caught up with him.

She waited until he stopped rolling and grabbed the front of his T-shirt.

"What happened?" she asked, gasping for breath between words.

"I don't know what you're talking about," he replied. "Let go of me."

She bunched his T-shirt tighter in her hands. "Not until you tell me what happened. Where's my father? Where's Professor Austin?"

"Professor Austin's where he always is. Why don't you go talk to him. I can't tell you anything." He tried to kick her, but Nick had too much leverage. She leaned closer and put her knee on his chest.

"I'm not letting go until you tell me what happened," she hissed in his face.

"What's going on here?" a voice cut in.

Nick stood up to answer and Clawson twisted away and scrambled down the hill. Nick tried to follow, but the campus policeman grabbed her arm.

"You're letting him get away," Nick protested.

"Ma'am, if I may say so, it looked like you were the aggressor. Some of the students saw you chasing that boy."

"That was my younger brother," Nick lied. "I'd heard that he was cutting classes. I'm paying for his education and I guess I just got a little too mad. Sorry for the misunderstanding. You know how brother-sister relations can be."

The policeman looked like he didn't believe a word, but Clawson was out of sight. "Ma'am, you've got to learn to keep your domestic disputes at home where they belong."

"You're right, officer. I'm sorry." Nick was having difficulty assuming a contrite expression. What she really wanted to do was give the man a good punch. Next thing you know, she thought to herself, I'm going to bat my eyelashes at him.

"Perhaps you could help me find my little brother's advisor, Professor Austin?" She fluttered her eyelashes as she inwardly cringed. "I really am so worried about him flunking out. My brother, that is. His advisor's in the archaeology department."

The guard pointed to the building behind him. "Try up there, ma'am." He let go of her and tipped his hat.

Nick took a deep breath before she flung open the door to Austin's office. Startled, Reed Austin jumped up from his desk.

"Office hours are over," he snapped.

"Not for me, they aren't," she retorted. "You've got some explaining to do. Where's my father?"

He shook his head. "Where he's always been, I presume." He hastily scrawled something on a piece of paper and handed it to her. The paper said, "Play along and follow me."

"Now if you'll excuse me," he said loudly. "I have a class to teach." He brushed past her before she could say another word and plunged down the hallway. Nick strode after him.

He never looked back. He took a right turn and then a flight of stairs that led downward. They ended up in a basement, next to the old furnace that heated the building in winter.

Austin turned and enfolded Nick in his arms. "Nick, I'm so glad that you're all right."

"Reed." She disentangled herself. "What the hell is going on?"

"You're father is safe. He should be back in Albuquerque by now. I thought you'd been briefed. Nick, it's a government thing. They came while you were gone and took everything. We were all sworn to secrecy. We shouldn't even be talking like this."

"You're right, Reed. We shouldn't be talking like this. We should be back at Baptist Wash talking about how we are going to best preserve our finds and how soon we can publish. Instead, we're down here in this basement like a couple of school kids."

"Nick, I have my job to worry about."

"And I don't? Is that it?"

"I'm sorry, I didn't mean to sound like I was thinking only of myself. I meant that my office could be bugged."

"What did they want? Was it the documents?"

He shook his head. "They wouldn't say. All I know is that we were to forget about ever being in Baptist Wash; forget everything associated with the dig."

"I'm not letting this go. They took my documents and my Packard."

"Forget it. You know the government. It's all locked away somewhere by now, so you might as well face it. That's the last you'll ever see of any of it."

She shook her head. "I'm going to call my father and then I'm going to get to the bottom of this."

"If you're going to take that attitude, then I guess I'm going to have to help you."

"What about your job?"

He smiled and, again, Nick saw his face transformed. "To hell with it. Some things are just more important. If we're going to get anywhere, we can do it faster together."

2₅

Lamar Decker felt the hundred-dollar bill burning a hole in his pocket. Irma Slater's hundred dollar bill, he reminded himself as he turned off the airport road to park in front of the Pilot Café. He killed the engine and headlights but made no move to get out of the car.

Irma's specter had been riding with him the whole way. Irma and Decker's mother both. Both working on his conscience. *Give the money back*, his mother was still harping from the grave. *Do your duty. Help the poor woman for nothing.*

Justice for my baby, Irma added.

"I'm out expenses," he reminded their specters. Half a dozen phone calls, gas for the Dodge, plus two dollars for a pint of bootleg bourbon. A must, he'd been told, if he was going to get anywhere with ex–state trooper Will Jennings.

Decker stepped out into blue light from the café's blinking neon propeller and hurried inside. The man behind the beer bar bore little resemblance to the photo Decker had dug up. Fifty pounds did that.

Decker took the end stool, putting distance between himself and the three drinkers there ahead of him. Four counting Jennings, whose glassy eyes said he was his own best customer. Jennings must have been drinking all day. It was hard to get drunk on 3.2 beer.

"I'll have a draft beer," Decker ordered.

Jennings mopped the bar before putting down the glass.

Decker laid down a four-bit piece. The hundred was still intact. "Have one on me."

Jennings drew a beer and drained half of it without coming up for breath.

"Let me sweeten that," Decker said, opening his coat to expose his bottle.

Jennings's eyes lit up like a man who'd been saved from drinking dregs.

Another fifty-cent piece went down, along with enough of the pint to make them pals. By the time the pint was a dead soldier, Decker had the man's life story.

"A dirty deal, that's what you got," Decker concluded.

"You're damn right. I'd be a captain by now in the state troopers."

"With your own car," Decker prompted. "Maybe even a driver."

"It's time I bought you one," Jennings said, drawing drafts for everyone at the bar.

By tomorrow, Decker figured, the man would be out of work for drinking up the profits.

"You ought to get yourself a lawyer," Decker said. "Sue them for ruining your career."

"Ca-reer," Jennings echoed, not quite getting his tongue around the word.

"You could have been killed in that shoot-out. Hell, from what I hear, anyone going up against the likes of Knute and Nora is lucky to be alive. How many cops was it they killed?"

Jennings wet his lips, trying to lube them so he wouldn't slur his words. "Don't believe everything you read in the newspapers."

"What do you mean?"

Jennings leaned close. "I shouldn't be telling you this. My mouth's what got me into trouble in the first place. But hell, what more can they do to me? Meet me out in back, and I'll tell you the whole story."

Decker, sober as a judge, smiled to himself. Now he could keep the hundred.

26

Nora Slater reminded Nick of her own mother. At least the face in the old photographs did. Surprising, since the Nora pictured in the newspaper was twenty years old, and the Elaine Nick remembered was middle-aged and haunted by demons only she saw.

Nick snapped open her pocket magnifier and studied the microfiche screen more closely. Nora definitely had the same possessed look as Nick's mother.

The date on the clipping projected on the screen was May, 1939, spring. The headline read KNUTE AND NORA ANNOUNCE WEDDING PLANS. Nora should have been happy, not haunted. The announcement had run in the *Provo Courier*.

Nick had a desk to herself in the Utah Historical Society's reference library, a courtesy more to her father's reputation than her own, she suspected. The society was located in what had originally been the old Denver and Rio Grande Railroad station. Some of the original brass spittoons had been preserved during the renovation. Along with them, Nick imagined she could still detect old cigar smoke.

Austin was researching Knute and Nora at the university's library. Together, she hoped they'd come up with some explanation of the FBI's hard-nosed attitude concerning a sixty-year-old crime.

After an hour at the microfiche, Nick had charted Knute and Nora's three-year career, a long time for bank robbers considering Bonnie and Clyde's bloody spree lasted only twenty-one months. Until their final shoot-out, the newspapers had portrayed Knute and Nora almost as folk heroes. Bank robbers had often been idolized during the Great Depression, when banks were hated for foreclosing on poor people and the government was hated for supporting the bankers.

Nick smiled at a story labeling Knute and Nora "good, God-fearing folk, who want nothing more than to settle down and raise a family."

Suddenly, one of Elaine's diatribes echoed in her head. *Archaeology's no job for a woman. A woman should marry and have children. Look at me, do I waste my time out in the desert digging in a sand pile?*

No, indeed, Nick told her ghost. You lived your life with the curtains drawn, in a house as dark as your own thoughts.

Nick returned her microfiche to the librarian who'd just come on duty, a young woman whose nameplate identified her as KALLY TUCKER, SENIOR STAFF. Without the badge, Nick would have guessed her to be of high school age.

Nick rubbed her eyes and muttered, "I'm getting old," without thinking.

"The microfiche does that to everyone. I have some eye drops, if you'd like."

"What I need is some help. I'm doing some background work on Knute and Nora Deacons."

The librarian glanced at the researcher's sign-up sheet on her desk. Nick's was the only name.

"Dr. Scott, I thought your field was the Anasazi."

"That's my father, Elliot Scott."

Tucker's eyes widened. "Of course, I've been reading his work for years."

Since kindergarten, no doubt.

"I've gone through your microfiche," Nick said. "Do you have anything else on Knute and Nora?"

"They're referenced in maybe a hundred books in our collection. Could you be more specific as to what kind of information you're after?"

Nick had anticipated the question. "On a recent dig, I came across some relics dating from their final days. That's the period I'm trying to piece together, the events leading up to their deaths in 1940."

Chewing on her lip, the librarian began running her fingers over the spines of books shelved directly behind her desk. Her finger landed on a vacant slot and she clicked her tongue. "I thought so. We have a book of folktales and songs that includes Knute and Nora, but it's checked out."

"That doesn't sound helpful."

"I seem to remember a song about their last shoot-out."

"What I need is eyewitness accounts of the time."

The librarian smiled. "You're in luck, then. I think we've got tape. Let me check the computer."

While the librarian went to work with her mouse, Nick paced, fingers crossed, hoping she wasn't in for endless sessions of viewing personal histories. Usually, they consisted of hour upon hour of unedited, videotaped recollections with an occasional five-second burst of insight.

"Here we are," the librarian said. "Old newsreel footage that's been transferred to tape. I'll set you up with a viewing room down the hall. While you're watching that, I'll pull a couple of books from the archives."

The videotape magnified every scratch and imperfection in the old, grainy black-and-white footage, to the point where Knute and Nora's bullet-ridden bodies didn't look real. The blood, which was everywhere, could have been mistaken for ink stains. Only their sightless, fly-blown eyes told the truth of their deaths.

The footage had been taken shortly after the Green River

shoot-out in April 1940. A few years later, censors would have deleted the gory shots. The narrator, in the sanctimonious rhetoric of the time, spoke of a "just end to a savage reign of terror, proof that crime doesn't pay."

Nick remembered seeing similar footage of Bonnie and Clyde's death car, with narration equally pretentious.

She changed tapes, to one labeled *Knute and Nora's Last Bank*. "This is Provo's quiet Center Street," the baritone narrator announced, the pictures matching his words. "It was here, on a rainy morning, that Knute and Nora Deacons shattered the peace and tranquility of this God-fearing town with a blast of machine-gun fire that took three lives. Two police officers and one bank teller who left a widow and three small children were cruelly slaughtered." The camera lingered on body outlines and bloodstains, then swung toward the ceiling, which was pockmarked with bullet holes. "Witnesses said Nora was about to leave the bank when she fired her Thompson submachine into the ceiling as a warning of what would happen to anyone who followed them."

Interesting, Nick thought as the tape ran out, but no different from Dillinger or Ma Barker. In their cases, the FBI wasn't panting after the loot sixty years later, though to be honest Nick had no idea if any was still missing. Maybe it was the documents they were after. But that made no sense. How could the feds know they existed? And even if they did, their reaction seemed extreme. After more than half a century, who'd care anyway. History was rewritten all the time. FDR's reputation would survive, though tarnished.

The final newsreel toured Knute's boyhood home and interviewed his neighbors, all of whom said he was a nice young man who minded his mother. Nora's neighbors weren't so kind, using the euphemisms of the day to label her as a loose woman.

Kally Tucker returned with a stack of old-fashioned photo albums. "People donate these to us by the hundreds. Mostly they're just family portraits. It's sad really. The family history gets passed on for a couple of generations and after that nobody remembers who's in the photos anymore. That's when they come to us. Sometimes . . ." She patted the top album in the stack she'd laid in front of Nick. ". . . we get lucky and people have collected historical photographs instead of just family pictures. Knute and Nora are in this batch somewhere, I remember. Of course, their genealogy is probably recorded at the church's Family History Library up the street."

Nick sighed at the sight of five albums, each two inches thick.

"You're welcome to keep using this room," the librarian continued, "but I've got to get back to the desk. Let me know if you want to run a genealogical search. We can log on from here, using our computer."

In Utah, Nick knew, genealogy was a tenet of the Mormon Church. Its members were required to research their ancestors, enabling the dead to be raised to heaven through individual baptisms.

Two of the scrapbooks had velvet covers into which elaborate brass letters had been set, spelling in script, FAMILY ALBUM. The other three had French ivory covers, a kind of early celluloid used to simulate ivory; all were cracked and yellowed with age. The pages were as thick as cardboard to accommodate the photographs of the era.

Nick started with the French ivory albums because they didn't smell as musty as the velvet. Knute and Nora showed up in the second album she tried. Someone, maybe a tourist with a camera, maybe a lawman even, had been on the spot when the pair drove their getaway car into the town of Green River. The photographer's first snapshot showed a pickup truck, blurred by motion, as it reached a roadblock. Another shot showed the vehicle fully stopped.

Probably the cameraman was snapping off photos as fast as he could wind his film.

In the next snapshot, the car doors were open. In the next, Knute and Nora were outside the car with their hands up. After that, all the snapshots were of their bloody bodies, taken from various distances and angles.

Nick backtracked to the picture of them, hands raised. Her pocket magnifier revealed a shadowy smudge that could have been a pistol. Why raise your hands if you intended to go down shooting?

Forget it, she told herself. Don't waste time asking questions that can't be answered, not after sixty years.

One by one, she went over the photographs with her glass. The cameraman had been meticulous. A newspaperman? She shook her head in answer to her own question. Back then, reporters had used single-shot graflex cameras.

Snapshots like those in the album were the province of tourists with Brownies.

Crowd shots followed. In one, a group of policemen were standing directly behind the bodies like hunters proud of their kill. Another snapshot had caught civilians milling behind a sawhorse barricade.

Nick's breath caught at the final photo. A group of men in dark suits and wide-brim hats were standing near the death car. One of them, she recognized. Or thought she did. She adjusted her magnifying glass to the blur-point. The man who'd caught her attention bore a striking resemblance to J. Edgar Hoover, the legendary director of the FBI.

She flipped through the remaining albums, but Knute, Nora, and J. Edgar were nowhere else to be seen. Chances were all she had was a lookalike.

She went back to the Green River snapshots. Obviously, they had been snapped over a short period of time. That meant the J. Edgar lookalike had to have been on the scene during the shoot-out. But that made no sense. Knute and Nora had never made post office walls outside of Utah. Hell, they hadn't killed anyone until their last robbery. They were hardly in the same league as Dillinger or Bonnie and Clyde. So why would J. Edgar be there?

He wouldn't have. He . . .

Stop. You're making assumptions.

So get more facts, she told herself, and borrowed a computer to search the Historical Society's database.

Fifteen minutes of cross-referencing the FBI with Knute and Nora brought several hits. But none of them mentioned J. Edgar Hoover.

Nick shrugged. That would have been too easy.

Working from her field notebook, she entered names of the men who'd signed the FDR documents. Dana Koplin was a no-show, as was Jerold Thomas. But Gordon Hanover, unknown to the Smithsonian's computer as well, was a big hit in Utah. His name was mentioned in more than a dozen publications, one of them *Who's Who in Utah Banking*, which listed him as one of the state's most prominent bankers in the 1930s. He'd died in 1940.

She pulled up his obit from the *Provo Courier*. Hanover had been president of Provo's First National Bank when Knute and Nora robbed it. He was a graduate of Harvard University and a classmate and close friend of President Franklin D. Roosevelt. A hunting accident had cut short Hanover's life. "See related story," the obit concluded.

Nick searched for it, but a full run of back issues of the *Courier* wasn't on file at the Historical Society.

She checked her Smithsonian notes concerning the other two, Thomas and Koplin. Both had died the following year, 1941. They, too, had been friends of FDR.

"Two bad years in a row for the president," she murmured and leaned back to flex her fingers. So what? The trio was long dead, as was everyone else connected with Knute and Nora's last bank.

Then why wasn't the FBI saying, so what, too?

With the librarian's help, she logged onto the church's genealogy site and ran names, including Hyrum Boyle.

The only surprise there was that Knute Deacons and Boyle were second cousins. Neither of them had surviving relatives. Nora's mother, Irma, was presumed to have died in 1946 in a house fire, although the remains were never formally identified.

The *Provo Courier*'s obit included a photo showing Irma holding the hand of her ten-year-old daughter, Nora.

Provo was only forty miles to the south. She'd pick up Austin at the university and they could drive there for lunch.

27

FBI agent Curt Rawlings wondered who he'd pissed off. It had to be someone important, otherwise why was he stuck following archaeologists up and down the state? During a July hot spell yet. What the hell was the point? They'd retrieved the documents for the man named Harold, whoever the hell he was, and chased off the archaeologists.

During their pre-strike briefing, the special agent in charge had said, "This comes right from the top." Meaning, of course, the J. Edgar Hoover Building in D.C. "Top priority."

It was then his partner had nodded in Harold's direction and asked, "Why are we taking a civilian?"

"Haven't your read your file folder? Police officers were killed," the SAC had replied angrily. "Furthermore, you will be taking orders from this man."

Even the SAC had looked cowed in Harold's presence.

Rawlings blinked away the memory and glared at his partner, Ward Edwards, who was driving the unmarked Chevy, a stripped down model that screamed government car. Hardly the blend-in kind of vehicle called for in surveillance manuals.

Edwards looked totally unconcerned with their present shit assignment.

"The brass are pussies, you know that," Rawlings blurted.

Edwards shrugged as if to say he'd heard it all before.

"When word comes down from the Hoover," Rawlings went, "they all roll over and play dead."

"What do you expect. The SAC was jerking us off, like always. That's why they made him the SAC."

"What about Harold? Do you think he was jerking us off?"

"He gave me the creeps, that's what he did."

"Fucking-A." Rawlings tugged at his tie to loosen the pressure on his sweat-chafed neck. "For chrissake, turn up the air conditioning."

"It's wide open just like the last time you asked me," Edwards shot back.

Rawlings thrust his hand over the dashboard vent. "I'm getting hot air here."

"You signed for the car. You should have checked it."

"Watch it," Rawlings said, pointing to the road ahead. "She's slowing down." The Scott woman had led them right back to where they'd started from, the university. Without warning, she pulled alongside a red, no parking zone.

"Christ!" Edwards blurted, then swung the Chevy into a driveway, temporarily losing sight of the woman's Jeep, not that it mattered. The locator beacon attached to her car was working perfectly. Even so, Edwards immediately backed up to reacquire their target. Their cell phone interrupted the maneuver.

Rawlings punched the dashboard speaker, since policy decreed that agents use both hands at all times while driving during surveillance. Besides, this way they could both listen.

"This is Assistant Director Miles Craycroft."

Rawlings and Edwards exchanged wide-eyed looks. Rumor had it that Craycroft was the real power at the Hoover building. When he spoke, he spoke for the director.

"Gentlemen," he began, his placid tone causing Rawlings to release the breath he'd been holding, "I want there to be no mistake on this. As of now, you're off the case. Forget everything you've seen and heard. Return to your office for reassignment. Understood?"

"Yes, sir," they said in unison.

"Good day, then, gentlemen." Craycroft disconnected.

"What was that all about?" Edwards said.

"I don't want to know," Rawlings answered. He didn't like the word reassignment. The last time it had been said to him, he'd ended up in Utah.

Craycroft took a deep breath and wiped his sweating palms on his knees, destroying the crease in his trousers. So far, so good. He was following orders to the letter. Whose orders he wasn't quite sure. The director had seemed vague issuing them, as if he were only passing them on.

Craycroft swallowed hard and rewiped his palms, wet as ever, on his crisp, carefully pressed handkerchief. Relax, he told himself. Do your job. The director knew what he was doing. A man in his position didn't take orders, he gave them.

Craycroft smiled. He was a proven power broker. As a result, people practically kowtowed in his presence, a state of affairs he reveled in.

So why was he sweating?

He ran a hand over his head, half expecting what hair he had left to give up the ghost.

"Just do it," he murmured aloud, then cursed himself for his momentary lapse which was now on audio tape for all posterity.

He wiped his hands one more time and called the Virginia number on his secure phone.

Special Counsel Beverly Zeien was expecting his call and answered immediately.

"As you requested, our field agents have been recalled to their office in Salt Lake."

"When?"

"Not more than a moment ago."

"I asked for immediate confirmation."

"I just got off the phone with them," Craycroft said, a lie but not more than a sixty-second one. Maybe less. All he'd done was wipe his hands.

Craycroft waited for Zeien's response. When the silence grew unbearable he sucked a quick breath and said, "May I consider the Spider File closed?"

"I'll tell you when, Mr. Craycroft."

Beverly Zeien, a handsome woman in her early fifties, broke the phone connection and turned to the man sitting beside her. "Mr. Fisher, you've seen the research on the Scott woman. Modern archaeology, or whatever they call it, is her area of expertise."

Paul Fisher nodded. In dark brown corduroy sports coat with leather patches at the elbows, tan slacks and loafers, he looked like a middle-aged college professor, not the hired political gun who'd gotten senators elected. His head was shaved to hide a pattern baldness that made him look like a tonsured monk.

"She's been very tenacious in the past," Zeien said. "For that reason, I think it best she should be, shall we say, removed from temptation."

What a nice euphemism, Fisher thought, for six feet of dirt in your face.

"And her father and the other man . . ." He consulted a small notebook. ". . . Doctor Reed Austin?"

"No loose ends. That would be my recommendation."

God, how he loved lawyers, especially ones with titles like special counsel. They seemed to think their title and a few weasel words made them immune when the shit hit the fan.

"They're important people," Fisher said, choosing his words carefully. "The father in particular. He's known to my . . ." He searched for a nonspecific term that would keep the counsel happy. ". . . sponsor." No doubt her electronic recorders were making her happy, too. An hour from now they probably would be edited to make her sound like a Supreme Court justice.

Fisher said, "My sponsor, to whom you owe your career,

would remind you that sixty years have passed and that everyone concerned is dead."

"The original cast had died off, to be sure, but the mission continued. The Eight, as they liked to call themselves, continued to guide and enforce their private designs."

He smiled. She, too, would have to be tidied up if things got out of hand.

"The sooner this is cleared up, the better," she added.

Already in the works, he answered to himself but said only, "I'll pass that along to my sponsor."

In downtown Salt Lake, Agent Edwards pulled the Chevy into the Federal Building's underground lot. Behind them, the security gate lowered automatically. A mechanic in overalls and a greasy baseball cap was waiting for them, waving them toward the hydraulic lube-rack.

"She's overdue for service!" he shouted at them.

"So are we," Edwards said for his partner's benefit.

Rawlings grunted and wrote down the odometer's mileage on their trip-sheet as his partner maneuvered the sedan into position and switched off the engine.

The mechanic knocked on the window, gesturing at them to release the rear door locks. The moment Edwards complied the man adjusted his cap and climbed into the backseat, chuckled, and said, "Word is you two have been reassigned."

"Jesus," Edwards muttered, "that was fast."

"Yep. I hear the papers are already in the works, signed and sealed."

Edwards stared at the rearview mirror but could see nothing but the cap's visor. "And I suppose you know where they're sending us."

"If I had to guess, to hell."

Both agents turned to get a better look at him.

"I'm only the messenger." As he spoke the thought hit him that a messenger was also a herald. What symmetry. He raised his head so they could see his face.

"Is that you, Harold?" Edwards asked.

"Absolutely, with either spelling."

Laughing at his own joke, he shot them both in the head before they had time to utter another word.

28

Nick's cell phone rang in the middle of lunch. She left Austin munching his hamburger and stepped outside onto Provo's University Avenue to take the call. They'd opted for the Utah Café, directly across the street from the *Provo Courier*. The café, at least, was air conditioned. A plaque on the wall beside her said the building had been constructed in 1902 for R. R. Irvine and Sons, a dry-goods business.

"It's Elliot," her father said. "Where are you?"

"Provo." Underfoot, the sidewalk was hot enough to make her shift her feet constantly. "And how come you left without leaving me a word?"

"I left that to the FBI."

"I haven't seen a sign of them." Nick glanced around looking for suits despite the 90-degree temperature. "Unless they're disguised as BYU students."

"Somebody's got a lot of clout, so watch yourself. The president of the university has grounded me personally, as if I were his teenage son or some damned thing."

"Reed Austin got the same treatment from the chairman of his department. He's been ordered to stay away from Boyle's Twist. But I still don't get it. Why would anyone care after so long? Particularly the FBI."

"The next time you see an agent ask him."

"I always knew it would be a mistake to work for you. And this proves it. If I'd been on salary, I'd have been grounded, too."

"I always thought airplanes would get you killed," Elliot countered. "Now I have to add 1937 Packards to my worry list. If you hadn't found the damned thing, I'd be with my Anasazi right now. For all I know, someone's claim-jumping my petroglyphs as we speak."

"Yours and Reed's," she reminded him.

He grumbled. "And yours."

"Speaking of mine, have I received any mail?"

"I've set it aside for you."

"Where?"

"In the sanctum."

"I thought you never went in there. It's probably full of dust and cobwebs."

"There's more than spiders in there, let me tell you. I had the feeling Elaine was watching my every move. It gave me the creeps."

"For a man who digs up the dead, you surprise me."

"Elaine's not dead, she's inside my head."

"You, too?"

Elliot snorted. "Your papers are safe. I made sure before her ghost chased me out of there."

"Better you than me." What was there about her mother, Nick wondered, that provoked such emotion from both her and Elliot? Elaine had been a demanding, manipulative woman who had suffered from a debilitating disease. Neither daughter nor husband had recognized the illness, leaving Elaine to battle her depression alone and yet not alone. Both Nick and Elliot had suffered from Elaine's mood swings without understanding that the root cause was medical in nature. The old wounds still had not healed.

"Perhaps it would be better if you came home."

"If you're trying to get me out of here, forget it. I'm not leaving until I know what's going on. Until Knute and Nora are mine."

"Now you know how I feel about the Anasazi," Elliot said and hung up.

She fought down the urge to hurl her cell phone into the street. She wished that her father had chosen any other place than Elaine's sanctum to hide the documents. On top of everything else, her father hadn't sounded good. She could fly to Albuquerque and back in half a day. But that would probably make things worse. Elaine's ghost was too strong in that house. She wondered why her father still lived there.

If she returned to the house, she could imagine her mother's ghost picking up the same old argument, the last words ever to pass between them. Spoken at Shirley's Beauty Salon of all places, a weekly haunt of her mother's since time immemorial. There, Elaine had her graying hair returned to its original red, matching Nick's. She was careful to match Nick's hair style as well.

"It makes us look like sisters," Elaine liked to brag.

"My hair snarls," Nick had complained for years.

"You should be thankful for your natural curls," Elaine had answered from Shirley's chair while Nick, like a supplicant, waited her turn.

"Long hair attracts bugs," Nick persisted, "especially on digs."

"A young woman has no business in such places."

"We've gone through this before, Mother. I'm making it my life's work."

"We'll see."

"I'm nineteen years old, Mother, a sophomore in college."

"You know how badly I need you, Nick. What would happen to me without you? You can never leave me."

Always the same words from Elaine, the implied threat, for

as long as Nick could remember, sometimes supplemented with dramatics and razor blade props.

Nick had walked out then, hurrying down the street to Shirley's archrival, Helen's House of Hair, for something very near a buzz-cut.

When Elaine saw it, she looked as if she'd been betrayed.

Nick shuddered as if someone had stepped on her grave, not a healthy thought for an archaeologist whose bread and butter was the dead.

29

Nick and Austin sat side by side sharing a yellowed and crumbling edition of the *Provo Courier*, dated April 21, 1940. They were seated on metal folding chairs, hunkered up against on old library table in the musty basement of the *Courier* building, the only space that could be spared to house the newspaper's morgue. Dust motes hung in the stale air like fog.

What the *Courier* called a morgue, Nick called chaos. Cardboard boxes were stacked in ceiling-high rows, teetering on the verge of avalanche each time she slid one from the pile.

Hack, the morgue man, who looked twenty years beyond retirement, had wished them luck, and then left them on their own, shaking his head, while he stretched out on a canvas-backed cot. His only proviso was that they keep everything in chronological order, otherwise his life would be hell.

The *Courier*'s first report of Knute and Nora's death came from a stringer who'd been rushed to the scene in Green River. In what the newspaper had bannered as an exclusive interview, the stringer quoted a state trooper named Will Jennings. "They had their hands up, and were trying to surrender when the shooting started. I didn't seen any sign of Nora's famous Thompson machine gun."

"Interesting," Nick said. "Probably the stringer was still working the folk hero angle."

Austin shook his head. "I don't think so. They'd left a trail of bodies behind them."

"Maybe he was on deadline," she improvised, "maybe phoning in his report." She tapped the byline. "Let's see what else Lewis Meeks has to say in later editions."

The shoot-out was front page news for the next few days, but never again under Meeks's byline. And there were no follow-ups on Jennings, the state trooper. So Nick assumed the stringer hadn't been a professional, but someone indulging in wishful thinking that Knute and Nora were still Utah's Robin Hoods.

Strangely enough, there was little mention of the FBI, though the feds had been headline seekers since the days of Dillinger. And there was sure as hell no mention of J. Edgar Hoover.

"Why isn't the FBI mentioned?" Nick asked, as much to herself as Austin.

He waved at the dust motes and sneezed. "I don't think we're going to find any reasons here." As he spoke, the newsprint in his hand crumbled. "My allergies are going crazy."

"Maybe you ought to wait outside," she said.

"That'll be the day."

After a week, the story faded to an occasional back-page human interest follow-up, one of them featuring Nora's mother, Irma Slater, who claimed, in quotes, that "her baby was an innocent led astray," and that the police had no business shooting her.

By May, ten days after the shoot-out, Knute and Nora had

ceased to exist as far as the *Provo Courier* was concerned.

"Let's backtrack and see what Knute and Nora were doing before they hit Provo," Nick suggested.

Austin groaned but fetched another molting box, which wasn't in much better shape than the newspapers inside it.

"This place is an asthmatic's nightmare," he declared.

Three days before the Provo robbery, Knute and Nora had hit a bank in Brigham City, north of Salt Lake. The week before that, they'd robbed a bank in Tremonton, farther to the north. Obviously, the pair had been working their way south, but for some reason decided to bypass Salt Lake, the biggest city in the state, and hit Provo instead.

No one had been hurt in either Tremonton or Brigham City. In the latter, Knute had refused to take money from bank customers, all of whom were women. Or so the *Courier* reported.

"Interesting," Austin said, "but not relevant."

"It does show us that Knute was still playing Robin Hood, or pretending to. He still wanted to be thought of as a hero."

"So?"

"So why did he start killing people in Provo?"

"To answer that, you'll need a time machine."

Nick sighed and kept backtracking through the dusty newspapers. While she did that, Austin paced and blew his nose. After a while, her eyes began watering as well, but she kept at it, poring over the disintegrating pages.

Suddenly Gordon Hanover's name caught her eye, one of the signatories of the papers she'd found in Knute's Packard. Exactly one week before the Provo bank robbery, Hanover had made headlines. Provo's First National Bank, where he was president, was under investigation, amid rumors of embezzlement.

"No formal charges have been made as yet," the *Courier* reported, "but bank examiners are expected to be called in for a complete audit."

Nick went the other way in time, tracking the embezzlement story.

HANOVER DEAD, a headline read. On the day the bank examiners were scheduled to arrive, Hanover took a rifle into the woods behind his estate, ostensibly to hunt, wrote a note confessing his sins—in the *Courier*'s words—"and then killed himself."

The following day, just ahead of the examiners, Knute and Nora robbed the bank.

She read the highlights to Austin.

"Nice timing," he said. "The man signs a damning document and then shoots himself so he can't be questioned."

"Help me here." She divided the stack of newspapers in front of her. "Look for follow-ups on Hanover and the bank embezzlement."

He blew his nose again and went to work. "Here we are," he said a few minutes later. " 'Bank Examiners pronounce Provo First National financially sound.' "

"And?" she prompted.

"And nothing. That's the gist of it."

"No charges?"

Austin shook his head. "Maybe the family paid back whatever had been taken in return for charges being dropped. Besides, you can't prosecute a dead man."

"Keep looking."

Austin's groan turned into a wracking cough. "My sinuses say no."

The sound brought the morgue man to their side with the comment, "That's why they call me Hack, working with all this dust. Nowadays, I wear a filter over my nose when I'm sorting papers down here."

"Now you tell us," Austin wheezed.

"Maybe you can help us," Nick said. "We're researching a man named Gordon Hanover and—"

The morgue man interrupted. "I thought you were after Knute and Nora Deacons."

"The name Hanover came up."

He shrugged. "Hanover's a prominent name here in Provo. What do you want to know?"

"Any kind of background on Gordon Hanover, a banker who killed himself back in 1940, would help."

Hack scratched an earlobe. "I used to know this stuff, but now . . ." He gave up on the lobe to shake his head. "I don't trust my memory, so we'll have to check what I call the church files, what with them being so keen on genealogy. We don't have many stored down here, but what we do have are prominent locals. The Hanover you want goes back a long way, so I'm not making any promises." He ambled over to a filing cabinet, unlocked it, and began rooting inside.

By now Austin's nose had stuffed up completely and he was breathing through his mouth.

"Why don't you wait for me outside," she told him.

He left without argument.

"You're lucky," the morgue man called out. "We've got clips." He held up a letter-sized brown envelope.

The envelope held photocopies of two stories. The first, a feature dated in pencil, June 1923, told of Hanover's triumphant return to his hometown after graduating from Harvard. The second clipping was dated 1939, with no month indicated. It reported that he and his wife, Emily, were off to the nation's capital, Washington, D.C., to visit Hanover's college classmate and now president of the United States, Franklin D. Roosevelt.

"President Roosevelt," the *Courier* went on, "was calling on friends and Harvard classmates to act as advisors during this time of international crisis. In addition to our own Gordon Hanover, Jerold Thomas and Dana Koplin, both of whom have been visitors to our fair city, have also been invited to the White House as advisors."

On a whim, Nick asked the morgue man to run the names Koplin and Thomas through his card catalog.

"Are they local?"

"I don't know, but they're mentioned in connection with Hanover in the clip you gave me."

He rummaged. "Jeez, you are lucky." He handed her another envelope. This one contained a brief wire story, the original copy by the looks of it. Thomas and Koplin had died in an airplane crash while on presidential business. The date was a week after Knute and Nora's shoot-out in Green River.

Nick made fresh copies of everything and then asked, "Does Hanover have any surviving relatives here locally?"

"I guess it is your lucky day, because I'm the only one around here who goes back that far. His children moved away after the scandal. Not that you could blame 'em."

"Where did they go?"

He shook his head. "No idea except for Gordon Junior. He turned hermit and moved up into the mountains. Town of Kamas, I heard, but that was years ago. If he's still there, it's an easy drive from here up the old highway."

30

In Washington, D.C., Paul Fisher answered his special phone, installed for the duration of this operation, a line that was completely secure. Only two people had the number. Only one would have the need to call.

"Yes," Fisher said.

"I've delivered the message. Retirement for two, courtesy of Harold."

"Any problems?"

"Only a mechanic. I had to borrow his overalls."

"Are we talking about a third retirement?"

"He's in a better place, that's for sure."

Fisher winced and hung up. The goal was everything, he reminded himself. Keep focused on that. The end justifies the means. Even so, the Spider File terrified him.

To calm himself, Fisher began pacing the length of his forty-foot office. He was oblivious to the individually spotlighted paintings, each framed in 22-karat gold, that hung on the walnut-paneled walls. There was a portrait by John Singer Sargent and California landscapes by Maynard Dixon, Edgar Payne, Conrad Buff, and Reed Farrington. The antique Bidjar rugs underfoot might as well have been dirt for all he cared. They were the trappings of his boss, Nelson Bishop III, known to his associates as Three-B, whose good taste and money had been inherited from his father Nelson Bishop, Jr., who owed the same debt to his father, the original Nelson Bishop, a robber-baron rivaling Carnegie and Rockefeller. With bloodshed and violence to prove it. Junior's hands hadn't been that clean, either. He'd broken unions, and necks when need be, forced competitors to the wall, one to suicide—though how he managed to shoot himself in the back no one knew to this day—in his quest for power and wealth.

It was Nelson Bishop, Jr., who'd hired Fisher, a public-relations guru, to clean up his image. By then Junior was sixty years old with a young wife who wanted not only respectability but an American title, senator or governor at the very least.

That's where Fisher came in. But you could buy only so much good publicity. There were holdouts, like the hardnosed journalists at the *New York Times* and the *Washington Post* who had long memories when it came to the name Bishop.

Fisher remembered the day he'd gone to Junior with the bad news, that the name Bishop couldn't be laundered like money. At best, Fisher had figured, it would be his last day as an employee. At worst . . . He shuddered at the memory. The Bishops had a reputation for making men disappear.

"There's a chance we could get you elected mayor," Fisher had said. "I can buy most of the papers and TV stations. Getting you elected to Congress is a long shot. Beyond that, we haven't got a chance in hell."

Junior had surprised him, then, clapping an arm around his shoulder. "I already own the mayor and governor, so what's the point? My father liked to brag he owned presidents. I saw him with two of them, so maybe it was true."

And your wife? Fisher wanted to ask. She was the one who wanted to live in the White House or the governor's mansion.

Junior just may have sensed the unspoken question. "We'll buy ourselves a couple of senators and invite them to dinner. That ought to make my wife happy."

"Yes, sir."

"And keep working on my image," he'd said. "Charities, things like that. My wife loves seeing our names in the paper. Spend whatever it takes."

A fortune had been spent, but not enough to cut into the ever-growing Bishop empire, so that by the time the third Nelson Bishop came to power the family name was synonymous with good works. The pension fund money had long since been laundered, so had the Vegas investments. Three-B's name was spotless.

Fisher gave up pacing to stand in front of the Sargent portrait. There, in subdued earth tones, stood Nelson Bishop, Sr., 1880–1944. He'd been forty when Sargent painted the portrait in 1920, a handsome forty, a man with a commanding presence. It was a good likeness, Fisher had been told by those who'd known the old man, but Sargent, being a great artist, had seen inside the man and exposed his ruthlessness in the eyes that held you in the same way a snake's gaze paralyzed a bird. Junior's eyes had carried the same message.

But what about Three-B? Was he tough enough and ruthless enough to go all the way, as Fisher was prepared to do? If not, Fisher was in big trouble.

He returned to his desk and stared at Three-B's silver-framed photograph. Other men in the organization had pictures of their wives and children in their offices. Fisher wanted nothing to distract him from his job, that of making Nelson Bishop the Third the next president of the United States.

Three-B had once kidded him about the photograph. "I'm not an icon, you know."

"You are. I've made you one."

Fisher knew people whispered behind his back. That he had no life other than the Bishop Foundation, not even a wife. "He's fifty years old, for God's sake, and not married," he'd watched them say on the video security system. "You know what that makes him." Wink, wink. So what if they thought he was homosexual. Their ignorance gave him an edge.

Fisher smiled to himself, imagining people picturing him as a pansy. That way, they wouldn't see his teeth until they'd already been eaten. And he'd eat anybody who stood in the way of his goal.

He laughed out loud. Power was better than sex, and so was money for that matter. The money, he already had in salary and stock options. The power would come when President Bishop named Fisher chief of the White House staff.

He pointed a finger at the silver-framed photograph and said softly, "Would you vote for this man?"

Why not? In the past five years, the Bishop Foundation under Three-B's stewardship had sunk billions of dollars into environment projects, literacy programs, scholarships, and worldwide health clinics. Strangely enough, to Three-B philanthropy wasn't a means to an end. He enjoyed doing good work. Which sometimes made Fisher wonder where Three-B had gotten his genes.

Fisher shook his head. Could good works and ruthlessness go together?

He slipped into his chair, which contained a built-in massage mechanism, and stared out at the nation's capital. His office overlooked the Potomac, though at a distance, and had the second best view in the Bishop Building. The structure had been built by Junior Bishop to house his lobbyists. It still held lobbyists, though these days they were dedicated to the foundation's good deeds.

The foundation itself was headquartered in Los Angeles, where Three-B also kept a home, following Fisher's advice that California was the perfect political base. When in Washington, as now, Three-B had offices and a five-bedroom penthouse in the Bishop Building.

Fisher, housed on the floor below, picked up his internal phone, and asked for a meeting with Three-B.

"Certainly, Mr. Fisher," said Bishop's secretary. "Just let me check the schedule." After a brief pause, she added, "Would ten minutes be acceptable?"

"Fine, thank you."

"Don't forget," the secretary added. "He'll be on his way to

Los Angeles in an hour. The handicapped children's benefit is tomorrow night."

"I won't," Fisher said, since he'd set it up himself. The ultimate in photo-ops, if he did say so himself.

Ten minutes later Fisher was ushered into Bishop's office. With him was Ken Ward, head of the foundation's environmental arm.

"I'm glad you're here, Paul," Bishop said, grabbing his hand as if they hadn't met in a long time, though it had only been two hours since the midday briefing. "A problem's come up and I want you to sit in on this." He nodded at Ward. "If you'd be so kind as to recap the situation, Ken."

Ward's swallow was loud enough to hear. "As you know, this year's environmental prize was awarded posthumously to Loren Hansen, a Canadian, who caught the oil companies polluting rivers near his home. He got himself shot doing it, if you'll remember, and so far no one's been brought to justice."

"I don't see the problem," Fisher said.

"You will," Bishop responded, then gestured at Ward to continue.

"We've just discovered that one of our overseas companies, Bishop International, owns a great many shares of the oil company responsible for the pollution, and quite possibly Hansen's murder."

Bishop looked at Fisher expectantly. Fisher said, "How much of an investment are we talking about?"

"It was worth fifty million before we awarded our prize," Ward answered.

"And now?"

"With our help, the late Mr. Hansen brought the oil company to its knees. Our shares are now worth ten million, give or take, depending on market fluctuation."

"Jesus," Fisher murmured, "that's a forty million dollar loss."

Bishop gestured impatiently. "You're missing the point, Paul. I've just ordered Ken to sell all our shares. Give them away, if that's what it takes. But I want our hands clean on this."

Fisher checked his own hands. They hadn't been clean since Nelson Bishop, Jr. hired him more than twenty years ago.

Ward stood up. "The market closes in an hour."

Bishop nodded. "Dump them and give whatever's left to charity."

"Which one?"

Bishop looked to Fisher, wanting his input, a good sign. Fisher calculated what would give maximum media exposure. "The homeless, right here in Washington to start with. We might need to expand the program later."

Bishop's nod of approval sent Ward on his way. As soon as the soundproof door closed behind him, Bishop said, "I know that look of yours, Paul. Something's on your mind?"

Fisher took a deep breath. Now was the moment to see just what Bishop had inherited from his forefathers. "The Spider File has been activated."

Bishop looked blank. "Should I know about that?"

"It dates from your grandfather's day. Your father had a hand in it, too."

"You haven't answered my question. Should I be concerned?"

Fisher had been anticipating that question for days. Full deniability was always best when it came to politics. But to achieve that, Bishop would have to be kept in the dark.

"Possibly not," Fisher said at last, "but there's always a chance the truth could come out."

"What truth and what does it have to do with me? My father's been dead two decades, my grandfather six. A grandfather I never met, I might add."

"The Spider File goes back to 1940."

"I wasn't born then."

Mentally, Fisher crossed his fingers. "If it gets out, it could kill your chance at the presidency."

Bishop looked stunned. "Before he died my father told me that you knew all the family secrets."

Fisher said nothing, assessing Bishop's eyes, looking for the ruthlessness Sargent had caught two generations ago.

"He said you could be trusted," Bishop went on.

"I can make you president."

"I don't want it for the same reasons as my father. It's the only way I can help this country."

"Maybe so," Fisher said, "but we're going to have to use your father's methods if you're to take up residence on Pennsylvania Ave."

"You said *we*."

"A joint effort, I'm afraid, starting with a full briefing on the Spider File."

"Why don't we discuss it on the way to L.A."

Fisher nodded. Bishop's private jet had just been swept for bugs, not that they'd be very effective competing with the roar from four jet engines.

Bishop stood up to indicate they should be on their way. "We'll have dinner on the plane."

If what I have to say doesn't kill your appetite, Fisher added to himself.

31

Nick drove while Austin navigated. The easy drive to Kamas turned out to be a thrill-ride on a narrow road with crumbling shoulders. Even in July the Uinta Mountains were covered with snow, their steep granite peaks criss-crossed with crevices of ice. The sharpest crags looked as if they'd been thrust up through the earth's crust during a violent eruption.

These mountains are like temples, she thought. They marked the entrance to Utah's high country, a quarter of a million acres containing peaks never climbed by man, unnamed lakes, and places seen only from the pressurized cabins of airplanes seven miles up.

The town of Kamas, population less than a thousand, lay at the base of the Uinta plateau, at an elevation of sixty-five hundred feet. From there, the highway climbed another four thousand feet before it crossed into Wyoming.

The area, the guide book said, had a semiarctic climate with snow a possibility year-round, but today the afternoon skies were clear.

When Nick and Austin left the car and climbed the steps of the Kamas Inn they were instantly out of breath from the sudden altitude change.

"Don't worry," the clerk said, watching them pant, "the altitude does that to everybody. I hope you're not looking for a room. We're booked up. Fact is, our season is very short here. Five months if we're lucky."

"We're looking for Gordon Hanover."

The clerk laughed. "Nine days out of ten I'd tell you I never heard of him. Fact is, folks around here are very protective of Gordon's privacy. But today he's in town having one of our home-cooked meals."

The clerk nodded toward the dining room. As far as Nick could see there was only a single diner, a man who looked to be in his seventies, dressed in jeans, a heavy red-flannel shirt, and lace-up boots. His long white hair and beard reminded her of a movie mountain man.

"I'll see if he's in the mood to talk," the clerk said and hustled into the dining room, where he bent close to Hanover and whispered something.

Hanover immediately looked her way, his eyes traveling up and down before he smiled.

The clerk returned to say, "I figured right. Gordon's never been one to turn down a pretty woman." He touched the side of his head. "A lot of people think Gordon's crazy, what with his funny notions. Will you two be wanting a meal?"

Until that moment Nick hadn't realized she was hungry. "That sounds good."

Austin nodded to say he was game.

"Seat yourselves, then. I'll bring menus."

"Mr. Hanover?" Nick asked when she reached the table.

He rose to greet her, bowing slightly, dispelling the mountain man image. Behind him, a large picture window looked out on the mountains. Two smaller windows were open to the crisp air.

Nick introduced herself and Austin. "We're archaeologists," she added.

"The last person came asking for me was a reporter, wanting to dig up the past. Now here you are, people who do nothing but dig up relics like me. You might as well sit down." He indicated the vacant chairs at his table.

The clerk-turned-waiter arrived with menus.

"I'd go with the special, if I were you," Hanover said. "I always do."

Nick eyed his plate, meat loaf. "I'll have the special."

"Make that two," Austin said.

The waiter left.

"Now," Hanover said, going back to his meat loaf without taking his eyes off Nick's figure, "I don't think you're here about archaeology."

"It started out that way," she said and then, with Austin's help, they recounted their dig in Boyle's Twist that started with the Anasazi and ended with Knute and Nora's Packard.

"I'll be damned," Hanover said when they finished. "I used to see pictures of that car when I was a boy. I used to wish I had one until they robbed my father's bank. They robbed it the day after my father was murdered."

Nick glanced at Austin, whose shoulder moved in an almost imperceptible shrug of skepticism.

Hanover picked up on it. "I know what you're thinking. Most people do. My mother thought the same thing, but she stopped talking about my father and told me to do the same. Someone threatened her, though she never told me about it until she was dying. By then it was too late to do anything."

To Nick, the likelihood of murder seemed remote. On the other hand, the bank investigation had been dropped.

She said, "Who made the threats?"

"I never knew, but there were police everywhere, I remember, for days, searching the house." He chewed for a moment, his eyes closed as if searching the past. "Some of them didn't have uniforms. Could have been lawyers, maybe. I figured it had to be one of them."

"What about FBI?"

"Anything's possible. Hell, I was a kid, remember, ten years old. One day I was playing with my friends, the next I was the son of a criminal and an outcast, shunned."

"Why do you think your father was murdered?" Nick asked.

"I don't think, I know."

Nick looked into the old man's eyes and saw nothing but conviction. She nodded for him to continue.

"He was supposed to be pheasant hunting. I remember him taking his shotgun."

Hanover paused, toying with his fork. "Our house backed right up against the woods, so all he had to do was climb the fence and walk maybe half a mile. I'd gone with him often enough, so I knew there were plenty of pheasant around."

Austin gestured impatiently but Hanover wouldn't be hurried. "You see, any fool knows you hunt pheasants with a shotgun. But the medical report said a deer rifle killed my father, the thirty-ought-six that was found beside him."

"Did he own such a gun?" Nick asked.

"Oh, yes, it was his all right, but I saw him take the shotgun. It came from his gun rack. Trouble was, the shotgun was missing. It's still missing as far as I know, because I have all my father's guns, even the ought-six, just about the only inheritance I got."

"Did you tell that to the police?" Austin said.

The old man nodded. "They said I must have been mistaken. They said suicides do crazy things, and that I'd better not start thinking crazy things, too. Otherwise something might happen to me."

"Are you saying they threatened you?"

"That's how I took it. I was a kid, remember, I was scared to death. When I told my mother about it, she told me to keep quiet, because there was nothing we could do. She died when I was in high school. When I was old enough, I moved up here in the mountains, where my dad used to take me when I was a boy. I feel safe here."

"Has anybody threatened you since?" Nick asked.

He shook his head. "It's ancient history. You're the first person to be interested in years."

"Why are you talking to us now?"

His eyes openly admired Nick's figure. "Maybe I'm not as harmless as I look. Maybe I'm looking for another wife."

She winked at him. "You don't have the stamina for someone my age."

"My last wife said that, too, and she's long in the ground."

Hanover gave up on Nick's figure to stare up at the rugged Uintas, where thunderheads were massing. "I hope you're going to cause trouble for the bastards who killed my father."

"If they're still alive, you mean."

"I'm here, aren't I?"

"Didn't you ever try to get at the truth yourself?"

"When did I have time? After my father died, my mother moved to Salt Lake and got a job. I got a paper route. There was no money for college, so I went in the army. I put in twenty to earn my pension, not much but enough for a cabin up by Mirror Lake. It's ten thousand feet up there, and we're snowed in six months of the year, except for snowshoes and snowmobiles."

"In your place," Austin said abruptly, "I would have hired a private detective."

Hanover snorted. "One came around once, asking questions, a seedy looking guy."

"Here in Kamas?" Nick asked.

"Hell no. That was years ago, before we moved out of Provo."

"What was he asking about?" Nick said.

Hanover stroked his beard as if searching for crumbs. "He was probably after the missing bank money like everyone else, but my mother sent him away with a flea in his ear."

Their food arrived. Nick picked at it for a moment before saying, "The newspaper said your father left a suicide note, confessing."

Hanover grimaced. "Pure bullshit. They showed it to my mother. It was typed. My father took great pride in his penmanship. I still have some of the postcards he sent from a banking trip to California. He wrote in copperplate script."

"How much money was missing from the bank?" Austin asked.

"There were all sorts of figures. The police blamed the confusion on Knute and Nora." Hanover touched the side of his nose. "My father took me aside when the *Courier* printed its first story. He told me not to believe what people would be saying about him. He said fifty thousand had gone missing, and he had someone in mind."

"Who?"

"He never said, but Knute and Nora came along and robbed the bank, so there's no telling what they took and what was already missing."

Nick speared a chunk of meat loaf and chewed thoughtfully. The money was gone, no matter what its amount. But the documents weren't.

She swallowed and said, "Was anything else stolen from your father's bank, except money?"

"Like what?"

"We found documents in Knute and Nora's Packard."

Hanover shrugged, obviously mystified.

Lightning flashed and thunder boomed, almost simultaneously. A breeze coming through the open windows carried the smell of ozone. The sky, blue when they arrived, was now a solid mass of surging thunderheads. Rain was beginning to fall.

Hanover checked his watch. "It rains like clockwork in these mountains." He stood. "It's time I started back, before a road washes out and I have to hoof it."

Nick stood, too, as did Austin, though he was still eating.

Nick said, "We understand your father was a friend of President Roosevelt."

"He was proud of that, even though he was a Republican. But that's Utah for you. Around here, Democrats are as scarce as non-Mormons." He chuckled.

"Did they correspond?" Nick persisted.

"The police took away all my father's personal papers, but he must have because he used to show me letters with the White House emblem on them. The police are bastards, you know that. I remember my mother crying when they accused my father of being in cahoots with Knute and Nora. Thinking back on it, that doesn't make any sense. If he'd arranged for the robbery, why kill himself? Once the money was gone there was no way to prove embezzlement or anything else. No, sir." He shook his head sharply. "It was murder. It had to be."

32

"**What now?**" **Austin said** as they climbed into the Jeep. The rain had turned to slushy snow. Three hours ago, when they left Provo, the temperature had been in the mid-90s. "Even if the old boy's right and his father was murdered, everyone connected with it will be long gone."

"We won't know until we try finding them," Nick said.

Austin, who was behind the wheel, shook his head in exasperation. "What do you have in mind?"

"A trip back to Provo."

He made a face. "My sinuses won't stand another session at the *Courier*."

"I want a look at the police records and the coroner's report if we can get hold of it."

"From 1940?"

"Just drive before we get snowed in."

Grumbling, Austin started the car, switched on the heater, and headed back the way they'd come. So far, the snow wasn't sticking to the two-lane asphalt. Even so, he drove hunched over the wheel, his lips moving occasionally as if he were talking to himself.

He didn't speak aloud again until they'd lost enough altitude for the snow to turn back into rain. "Murder doesn't make any sense to me. No one had motive."

"You heard the man," Nick said. "The real embezzler."

"The paper said Hanover was the one under investigation."

"Papers can be wrong."

"Most of the time, I'm sure. But I still don't buy it. Whatever the case, it looks to me like Knute and Nora took the evidence with them."

"Did I tell you about J. Edgar Hoover?"

Austin's sigh reminded her of Elliot when he'd been under assault during one of Elaine's verbal barrages.

"He was in one of the Green River photos."

"I didn't see him in the *Courier*."

"I found a series of snapshots in an old photo album at the Historical Society."

"Was he identified as such?"

"He looked like J. Edgar Hoover."

He glanced in the rearview mirror, checking for traffic, and then slowed until he could take his eyes off the road for a moment. When he did, he looked at her, his eyes narrowing. "You're on my home ground now, Nicolette, and I've never heard of Hoover being personally involved in the hunt for Knute and Nora."

"Maybe he wanted to keep a low profile."

With a snort, Austin went back to watching the road. "He was always high profile when it came to catching criminals."

"Maybe he was there to protect the president."

Austin wiped a hole in the windshield mist, then switched the blower to maximum. "I'm sorry, Nick. It was 1940. We weren't at war yet. Your documents had to be fake as far as I'm concerned."

"We've been over this before. There was war in Europe, remember."

"Okay, so war in the Pacific was inevitable."

"Maybe Hoover knew what the Japanese were up to."

"I didn't see his name on any of the documents."

"Maybe Hoover was in Green River on behalf of Roosevelt. Maybe that's why the FBI came down on us so hard. Maybe they're still protecting them both."

"Still following Hoover's orders sixty years later, is that what you're saying?"

"Maybe."

"You've got to be kidding. Politicians are vicious. The Republicans would love nothing better than to destroy the image of FDR and his New Deal, but—"

She interrupted him. "How do you explain the FBI's interest after all these years?"

"They're anal retentive."

"Aren't we all."

Austin chuckled. "You're just like your father, you know that."

"I'm not sure you know either of us well enough to comment," she shot back.

"I meant that as a compliment."

"Just drive."

Since the day she'd announced her intention to go into archaeology, everyone had compared her to Elliot. To the great man. To the grand old man of Southwestern archaeology. The comparison wasn't always spoken aloud. Sometimes it was innuendo, reflected in smiles, sometimes laced with envy, other times with a touch of pity, but always at her expense. And it would only get worse if she ever went to work for him. Then she would live in his shadow permanently.

Maybe Elaine had been right. Maybe archaeology wasn't a suitable job for a woman.

Nick smiled at the thought. Elaine had always thought of archaeology in terms of ruining her nails on dirt-encrusted artifacts, or callusing her hands digging in ancient graves. To Elaine, perfect hands were the mark of a lady.

Nick eyed her own unpainted, bluntly clipped nails. "What would you say now, Elaine?" Nick asked, her thought slipping out.

She glanced at Austin, expecting him to seek an explanation. But he was back to hunching over the steering wheel, his lips moving as he carried on his own private conversation.

They came out of the rain into sunshine and steam began rising from the asphalt. Austin turned off the heater and rolled down his window. Nick did the same. The warm outside air told her they were out of the mountains and in summer again.

"Do you think I'm crazy?" she said after a while.

"I'm here with you, aren't I?"

"Did my father ask you to stick close?" she asked, suddenly suspicious.

He pulled onto the shoulder and stopped. "The FBI tossed me out just like they did you. That pissed me off, but there's nothing I can do about those Anasazi petroglyphs at the moment. A week from now, when things have cooled off, I just might sneak back into Boyle's Twist and have another look. Until then the best way I can think of to screw the FBI is to go after Knute and Nora with you."

"You haven't answered my question about Elliot."

"You're better looking than he is for one thing."

"And for another?"

He leaned over and kissed her.

She pushed him back. "Reed, I find you very attractive, but I think this isn't the time or place. After this is all over, who knows. Right now I want to concentrate on unraveling this mess."

"Yes, ma'am," he said and swung the Cherokee back onto the highway.

Nick smiled to herself. Knowing a man was attracted to you in advance made things a lot easier if you decided to put Elliot's theory to the test, that unearthing a fine artifact was better than sex.

33

Harold grumbled to himself, wondering why the archaeologist's car had stopped. Now that they were out of the mountains, the highway had stopped switching back and forth and he could see the empty road ahead for a mile at least. His eyes were good, better than twenty-twenty, but it was the locator beacon attached to their car that told him they'd come to a halt. He did the same.

Maybe they'd stopped to fuck. Harold's last lady had been a backseat quickie, so why not them? Because, dummy, it was broad daylight and God knows what kind of Mormon laws they had against such things in Utah.

Harold had to take a piss, but he knew better than to get out of the car. The moment he did, they'd take off like race drivers sure as hell. Still, how far could they get? The Provo city limits were coming up in a couple of miles. After that, traffic would slow them down. And if they parked in the city before he caught up with them, what then? Then your ass will be in a sling.

Lucky he'd been on long distance surveillance. Otherwise they'd have spotted him for sure in that dump of a town, Kamas. What kind of people would live in a place where it snowed in July?

Ass sling or not, he opened the door, hand already at his zipper, when his cell phone rang.

"Yes, sir," he answered, knowing only Fisher would be calling.

"Where are you?" Fisher asked.

Utah, Harold was tempted to say. Where the hell do you think? But he settled for, "Playing long distance tag as ordered. We're headed back toward Provo at the moment."

"Things are taking a turn here. I may need your hands-on touch again, so move in for close surveillance."

"I don't like doing women."

"I'll get back to you before you leave Provo," Fisher said and hung up.

34

The duty sergeant at the Provo police station looked at Nick as if fitting her for a picture on a post office wall. Or maybe a straightjacket. Probably he was suspicious of anyone. His Kevlar inflated chest said as much.

But he listened intently enough before saying, "Lady, you've got to be kidding. Do you know how many cops have come and gone since 1940?" He nodded at the framed photographs of policemen on the wall behind her.

"The crime I'm talking about is embezzlement and a bank robbery where two policemen were killed," she explained further.

"In Provo?"

"You must have heard of Knute and Nora Deacons and their shoot-out here in town. It got them hunted down and killed."

"Nineteen-forty, right?"

Nick nodded that it was.

"I was never one for history, but cop killers!" The sergeant sucked air in disapproval, expanding his chest and stomach to button-popping proportions. Even when he exhaled his buttons remained at risk. His name, according to the plastic tag over his breast pocket, was Evans. "I don't remember the shooting myself, but you'll find a marble wall around here with the names of our honored dead, if that'll help you any, but we'd need a football stadium to keep records that far back. Sorry."

"How about a coroner's report for a 1940 suicide?"

Evans chuckled quietly. "Make that two stadiums and the BYU gym."

"Would anywhere else have records dating that far back?"

"The newspaper, maybe."

"We've been there already."

He scratched his chin. "How about the church library up in Salt Lake?"

"I'm writing a book," she lied, "so I need more than a death certificate."

"What kind of book?"

"Bank robbers of the Great Depression," she improvised. "I'll be featuring Knute and Nora."

"They got what they deserved," the sergeant said. "But I'm sorry I can't help you." He spread his hands in a gesture of helplessness. "These days, if it isn't in the computer it doesn't exist."

Nick looked at Austin for suggestions. His only answer was a shrug of frustration. She knew exactly how he felt.

"Dammit!" Nick blurted.

"If you were after something in the 1970s," Evans said sympathetically, "we might have a shot at it. Before that, forget it. If it hasn't been destroyed, chances were it wasn't kept in the first place. Or maybe not even written down, for all I know. My father was a Provo cop before me, and he doesn't go back as far as you're talking about."

Nick snapped her fingers. "Sergeant, you're a genius. We don't a need a policeman, we need an historian."

The sergeant looked blank.

"Who's the oldest Provo cop you know?" she asked.

Evans grinned, obviously relieved to know what she was getting at. "You're not just another pretty face, if you don't mind me saying so. Let me ask around."

He retreated out of earshot, got on the phone, and began making calls. Every once in a while, he'd nod, hang up and dial again.

Nick kept count. After the sixth brief conversation, he came back to the counter and rested his stomach against it. Nick crossed her fingers.

"I called some of the old-timers I know," Sergeant Evans began. "Nobody went back that far, you understand, and they sure as hell didn't remember your robbery, though Knute and Nora rang a bell."

He grinned roguishly and Nick knew it was safe to uncross her fingers.

"We did come up with a name. Chief Tuttle. You can see his picture on the wall over there."

The plaque underneath the austerely framed photograph read POLICE CHIEF BEN TUTTLE, 1955–1975. "He was on the force back in 1940," the sergeant went on. "That's the word anyway."

"He must be eighty by now," Austin said.

Evans ticked off the years on his fingers. "Closer to ninety, I'd say. If he isn't dead."

Austin rolled his eyes. "Don't you know for sure?"

"Sorry. He's not local anymore, so nobody's kept in touch."

"Where can we find him?"

"Orderville, Utah. With old Tuttle living there maybe they ought to call it Law and Orderville."

His laughter followed them out of the police station.

3₅

The pilot came on the intercom to say, "We're cruising at an altitude of thirty-one thousand feet and are presently over western Kentucky. The turbulence has subsided and from here on, the weather people tell us we should have a smooth flight all the way into Los Angeles."

To Fisher's way of thinking what the pilot called subsiding was as jarring as riding a motorcycle. Even the plush leather seats on the private 737, christened Bishop One, couldn't cushion the aerial undulations.

Fisher swallowed hard. Acid roiled in his stomach and his kidneys were verging on rebellion. There was a time when messengers delivering bad news were killed for their efforts. But Fisher didn't have any choice. Not now. Everything had to be told. He swallowed again. The worst Bishop could do was kill his stock options. No, worse would be Fisher's removal from power.

"I love it up here," Bishop said from the facing leather recliner. "Here I feel I have complete control over my life."

"When you're flying Air Force One you'll have complete control over the world," Fisher responded.

"We have to win the election first."

"I learned from a master, your father. 'Never put yourself in a position to lose, only win,' he said."

As one they swiveled their chairs to face yet another portrait of Nelson Bishop, Jr. This one looked back at them from the jet's carpeted wall. It was one of dozens of portraits Junior had commissioned in his lifetime. *None of them caught my essence*, Fisher remembered him saying once. *That's why I keep hiring artists.*

"If my father was so goddamned smart," Bishop said, "why did he stick me with a legacy like the Spider File?"

You haven't heard the worst yet, Fisher answered to himself. The Spider File had been Junior Bishop's deathbed revelation to Fisher, made only after Fisher had signed a blind contract, which, Bishop's attorney informed him before leaving the room, bound him for life.

"Did I ever tell you about the Peace Corps?" Bishop said.

Repeatedly, Fisher thought, but only nodded.

"I volunteered to serve my country and they sent me to Ethiopia to help increase farm production. Three of us were assigned to a small village. We did our best for two years, but it was hopeless. By the time I left the villagers were still starving. You know what I did, then?"

Only too well, Fisher responded silently.

"I came home and used some of my inheritance to turn their lives around. For me, that was the beginning of the Bishop Foundation. My father thought I was crazy. He said money was power and not to be squandered on peasants. Until that moment I'd never believed the stories I'd heard about him, or the books that had been written about him, either. He worshiped money, I don't."

Because you've got more than you could spend in two lifetimes.

The seat belt sign went out, despite the continued nonturbulent bounce. Bishop unbuckled immediately and began to pace in front of the portrait. As far as Fisher could see, the old boy's essence was there all right, like it was in so many of the other portraits, right down to the shrewd, unforgiving eyes. He compared them with Three-B's eyes. Take away the smile lines and they were dead-ringers, father and son. Fisher crossed his fingers. He hoped.

One of their two stewardesses arrived to ask, "Sir, when would you like dinner served?"

They'd already ordered ahead, Caesar salad, broccoli quiche, and fresh peaches for dessert. On the ground, it had sounded great to Fisher. Up here was another matter.

Bishop turned away from the portrait to look at Fisher. "What do think, Paul? Does fifteen minutes sound all right to you?"

Fisher nodded. He knew an order phrased as a question when he heard it.

"Good. It will give us time to finish our chat." Bishop smiled at the stewardess. "I hope that will give you enough time."

"Yes, sir," she said and retreated to the galley, closing the folding door behind her.

Bishop folded his arms across his chest and addressed the portrait. "Sometimes, I think I should have turned down my inheritance and gone out on my own. What do you think about that, Paul? What would have become of me if I'd . . ."

His voice trailed off, forcing Fisher to unbuckle and move closer to hear above the jet roar. Standing up seemed to amplify the plane's vibrations. They thundered up his legs and into his already queasy stomach.

"If I'd turned down my inheritance," Bishop continued, "the Spider File wouldn't be my worry. It would be somebody else's."

Fisher braced himself. There was no use putting off the inevitable. "You haven't heard it all yet."

"Good God. What you told me already was bad enough. My grandfather must have been crazy."

"Like a fox."

"You admire him, don't you, and you weren't even there to know him?"

"I guess I do."

Bishop turned from the portrait to face Fisher. "Why the name Spider File?"

Fisher shook his head.

"Does that mean you don't know or won't say?"

"Yes, that's right."

"No wonder my father trusted you." Bishop looked from Fisher to the portrait and back. "Do you know what he said to me once? 'Paul knows enough about this family to destroy us.'"

Fisher smiled weakly. That kind of knowledge could get a man killed.

" 'But I trust him with my life,' my father said. 'I advise you to do the same.' " Bishop snorted. "I pride myself on being my own man. Some of my father's advice I've taken, some I haven't. But I've never been uncertain about you. What I want to know now, though, is whether or not J. Edgar Hoover knew about the file."

Fisher had considered his answer well in advance. "As you'll notice, the file doesn't say."

"And what do you say?"

"I never spoke to Mr. Hoover."

"That's not exactly an answer."

Fisher took a deep breath. For Nelson Bishop III the presidency was within grasp. Good deeds had made him the darling of the media. Serving in the Peace Corps was just as good as being a war veteran. He was happily married and had never strayed. Through constant surveillance, Fisher knew that for a fact. He'd never used drugs. He'd never been arrested. There were no personal indiscretions, and no scandal except for the one he'd inherited. Which was more than enough to end his political career before it started. To avoid that, the Spider File had to be dealt with once and for all. Once that was accomplished, Bishop would realize his ambition, and so would Fisher, as White House chief of staff, the second most powerful man in the world. The man behind the throne was also safer, if for no other reason than he was out of the line of fire.

"Hoover is dead and moot," Fisher went on. "What we have

to address now is the problem of the Scott woman. She's got hold of this thing and won't let go. She and the other archaeologist."

"What can she do? You said the FBI has tidied up."

I had to tidy up after them, Fisher answered to himself.

"There are some things," Fisher said, "that you shouldn't know."

When Bishop started to object, Fisher rushed on. "Better you don't have to lie if reporters start asking questions."

Bishop's eyes narrowed as he considered what had just been said. Finally, he asked, "What happens if we ignore the whole thing?"

"Nelson Rockefeller wanted the presidency, but the Rockefeller name was stained too badly by his ancestors. The Bishop name wasn't much better until you came along. You've created a new image for yourself."

"I wasn't thinking about running for office when I started the Bishop Foundation."

"I know that, so do the American people. That's why our polls show that you're one of the few of the superrich that Americans trust. But if the Spider File goes public, all that changes."

Bishop went back to his seat and belted himself in. "I'm not sure I know what you want from me."

"Your approval to do what's necessary."

"What does that mean?"

"It means," Fisher clarified, "that you shouldn't ask."

Bishop said, "I don't want anybody hurt."

"Of course," Fisher answered. Now wasn't the time to bring up Harold. Let Bishop get used to one thing at a time.

"No violence, then?"

"They're archaeologists after all. It shouldn't come to that. The thing to keep in mind is what you'll be able to do for this country when you become president."

Bishop wet his lips. "All right, you have my permission."

And I have you saying it on my tape, not yours.

Fisher was suddenly hungry. When the stewardess served dinner, it was Bishop who only picked at his food.

36

Nick consulted the Utah guide she kept in the Jeep's glove compartment. Orderville, population 423, had been settled by the Mormon Church in 1864, and became an experiment in co-operative living. For ten years, all wealth was pooled and shared equally. Everyone wore the same home-spun clothing and ate at the same communal table. Then boom times came and people wanted to cash in. Cooperation gave way to capitalism.

As Nick and Austin turned off the highway all sign of the boom was gone. Main Street was a couple of motels, a café advertising "Mom's home cooking," and a rock shop. The drive itself, five hours from Provo in desert heat, had brought the Jeep's air conditioning to a shimmying standstill.

"I hope this is worth it," Austin

said when they parked. He looked as limp and dispirited as she felt.

Visions of cold drinks danced in her head as she stepped out of the Jeep's tepid interior and into an Orderville furnace. Their destination, a squat, one-story brick house tucked beneath an enormous cottonwood tree, looked cool in the shade. A roofed screen-porch ran along the front of the house.

They'd called ahead, and Ben Tuttle, Provo's long-retired police chief, was waiting for them on the porch, swinging back and forth on a metal glider that squeaked with every arc.

"The door's not latched," he called when Nick hesitated on the steps.

Wicker chairs had been placed facing his glider. He waved Nick and Austin into their seats and said, "You mentioned on the phone you wanted to talk about Knute and Nora's last bank."

Right to the point, Nick thought, a sharp-eyed cop even in retirement. Tuttle had to be well into his eighties, but looked more like a hearty sixty-five. His shoulders were broad, his stomach in check.

"I wasn't much more than a rookie when Knute and Nora hit town," he went on, eyes twinkling as he took in her figure. "But you must know that already. I'm betting you're here because I'm the only one left who can remember that far back." He grinned. "It's a good thing you don't want to ask me what happened last week, because my short-term memory's shot to hell."

"Why Orderville and not Provo?" Nick asked.

Tuttle chuckled. "Everybody asks me that. I always tell them it's cheap living here, especially when you're on a police pension. But the truth is the name appealed to me."

Nick looked over her shoulder at what passed for the center of town. "There's no bank to rob, that's for sure."

"There's no nothing to rob, young lady, unless you were desperate for small change."

"Call me Nick. It's short for Nicolette."

"Nicolette," he repeated. "I like the sound of that. You know what, Nicolette, I've been retired twenty-five years and

there are days when I still miss the excitement of police work."
He winked at her. "Listen to me, sounding like a big-town cop.
The fact is, police work is ninety-nine percent boredom in a
place like Provo, and one percent sheer terror."

He cocked an eye at Austin, who hadn't said a word so far.
"You don't look like an archaeologist to me. Neither does Nicolette." Tuttle snorted. "But then, I don't know as I've ever
met one before. I guess two at once makes this my lucky day."

Nick had the feeling Ben Tuttle had been very good at his
job, playing the innocent, like now, lulling his suspects while
his sharp eyes missed nothing.

"Now where were we?" he said with just the hint of a smile.
"Talking about archaeology, that's it."

"If you'd like," she said.

He laughed. "If I were twenty years younger, Nicolette, you
wouldn't be safe. To start with, I'd tell you those jeans have to
go. A woman, especially one as good looking as you, shouldn't
cover up her best parts."

Nick answered with a cold, hard stare that Elaine had helped
her perfect. *It always works on your father*, Elaine had insisted
during practice sessions.

Tuttle held up a surrendering hand. "Okay, I've been
warned. I'll stick to Knute and Nora." He closed one eye as if
taking a bead on the past. "They were a pair, they were. My
father followed their exploits in the papers. He even made a
scrapbook. He said he was doing it for me, because a cop had
to keep up on crime."

His eyes lost focus. Nick knew the look. Her father often
had it when Elaine came up.

Tuttle sighed. "Thinking back on it, I figure my father had
dreams of me capturing Knute and Nora one day, single-handed
of course. The trouble was, he was like everybody else back then.
He didn't see Knute and Nora as criminals, but just plain folks
getting back at those who'd done them wrong. 'It's the government and the greedy bankers,' my father used to say. 'Forcing
people to get by any way they can.'"

He leaned back in the glider and rocked for a moment, his
eyes closed, focused on his memories, Nick felt certain.

"What about their bank robbery in Provo?" she prompted after a while. "Were you there?"

He shook his head. "Like I said, I was a rookie in those days, so they had me walking a beat in the boonies. I didn't hear about the robbery until the end of my shift."

Wicker creaked as Austin shifted positions. "That seems strange, what with cops being killed in a small town like Provo."

"Funny you mention that. I saw the newsreels after Knute and Nora were killed. They showed the bank and where the bodies had fallen. But it never happened." He laced his fingers together, settled them on his stomach, and smiled at Nick's legs.

"Go on," Austin urged.

Tuttle's smile widened.

Nick exposed an inch of ankle, the best she could do in tight jeans.

Tuttle clicked his tongue at her and continued. "Like I was saying, a rumor got out that people were gunned down in that bank. A regular massacre, the radio called it, so the newspapers picked up the same story. I guess it was reporters making up tales to sell papers."

"It can't be," Nick said. "We've been through back issues of the *Provo Courier*, and there weren't any retractions."

Tuttle clicked his tongue again. "You should know better than that, Nicolette. Newspapers don't retract unless there's somebody threatening to sue them. Knute and Nora were dead, so that was an end to it."

"What about the dead cops?" Austin said.

Tuttle shook his head. "Like I said, it never happened."

The duty sergeant at the Provo police station hadn't remembered the dead either. Then again, who would after sixty years? Only an obsessed archaeologist, Nick told herself.

She said, "I got the impression that the shoot-out in Provo triggered the manhunt."

"Knute and Nora were always on our wanted list," Tuttle answered, "but you're right. When word got out about Provo, that cops were dead, every police officer in that part of the state was put on alert."

"I read about a second massacre at one of the roadblocks," she said.

"I don't know about that. I was on alert looking out for Knute and Nora, like everyone else, but I never left town. You ask me, once reporters start making up things, who's to say where they'll stop."

"Did anybody ask you about this before?"

"There was a lot of red faces at the time. Don't get me wrong. Knute and Nora got what they deserved, but the chief, name of Pat Keeley, called a meeting about the dead cops who weren't dead after all. 'Let's keep this to ourselves, boys,' he said. 'No use looking like we've got egg on our faces.' So we shut up about it."

"And it was the chief's idea?" Nick probed. "This man Keeley."

"There were a lot of brass around, I remember that." Tuttle eyed the inch of ankle she'd exposed like a man hoping for more.

"Mr. Tuttle," she said, "I think you can do better than that."

"I think you can do better, too."

"Next time I come through Orderville, I'll wear a skirt, a short one. That's a promise."

Chuckling, he slapped his knee. "Nicolette, you're a pistol." He glared at Austin. "You treat her right, you hear me, young man."

"Yes, sir," Austin said.

Tuttle nodded and went on. "The FBI was at that meeting, too. For all I know, they called it and Chief Keeley just went along. The gist of it was, the feds ordered us to keep quiet. Otherwise, they said, there'd be legal problems. They made it pretty damned clear our jobs were at stake. Since the chief didn't say otherwise, we figured the feds were speaking for him. Besides, nobody got hurt except Knute and Nora, and we weren't about to shed tears over the likes of them."

Nick checked her notes. "Did you know a state trooper named Will Jennings?"

He shook his head.

"A stringer for the *Courier* interviewed him right after the shoot-out in Green River," Nick added.

"Yeah, that rings a bell. I seem to remember someone getting into trouble over an interview. Could be that's why the feds clamped down on us."

"What kind of trouble are we talking about?" Nick asked.

Tuttle shrugged. "I don't know that I ever heard."

Nick thought for a moment. "There must have been scuttlebutt at the time, maybe locker room talk at the police station."

Tuttle shook his head. "I told you, the feds clamped down."

"A day or two went by between the time Knute and Nora hit the bank in Provo and the shoot-out in Green River."

Tuttle counted on his fingers. "Four days, I think. They must have been holed up somewhere."

"And you don't remember anything being said during that time?" she probed.

"Our meeting with the chief, the one with the feds, that was the night of the robbery." He took a deep breath and closed his eyes. "I can still see it. We met late, maybe ten o'clock, twelve hours after they hit the bank."

"The feds sure got there fast," Austin pointed out.

Too fast, Nick thought, for a small town bank.

No one spoke for a while, and Tuttle went back to rocking his squeaky glider. Finally Austin abandoned his chair and moved to the screen door, where he stood peering out at the town of Orderville. After a moment Austin spoke without turning around. "Law and Orderville, that's what your cohorts in Provo call this place."

"Suits me," Tuttle answered.

Still facing the town, Austin said, "Tell us about Gordon Hanover's suicide."

"I told you already. I was a beat rookie."

"His son says it was murder."

"Nothing to do with me," Tuttle answered.

Austin swung around. "Are you a hunter?"

Tuttle looked wary but said, "In my youth."

"Tell me, then, what kind of gun would you use to hunt pheasants?"

Tuttle stopped rocking and rose with a grunt, his hands bracing the small of his back. "A man my age needs his rest." He moved to the door into the house and opened it. "You should remember that, young man, in case you live so long."

Tuttle looked at Nick and bowed stiffly. "I was hoping to see you in that short skirt of yours, Nicolette, but . . ." He shook his head regretfully. ". . . I don't think I'll get the chance."

He disappeared inside without another word.

"I didn't like the sound of that," Austin said once they were back in the Jeep and driving away. "Do you think he was afraid to say anything?"

"I don't think he was afraid for himself," Nick said.

"Yeah, that's what bothers me."

37

On the drive back to Provo, Nick went over her notes. There were a few more names to be checked. Beyond that, she couldn't think of anything else to do. She relayed her thoughts to Austin, who was driving.

"Well?" she said after failing to get a response.

"I'm with Chief Tuttle. I want to see that short skirt of yours."

Nick ignored him. "The way I see it, we run the rest of the names through the genealogy library. After that, all we're left with is the Freedom of Information Act, and you know how Republican administrations hate that. We might get them to release those documents in time for our retirement."

"I'm surprised at you. Your father compared you to a pit bull. He said you never let go once you bit onto something."

"Surprised how?"

"You're forgetting the *Courier*. The stringer is one of the names you want to run, right?"

"Yes, Lewis Meeks."

"Let's start with his place of employment, then."

She nodded. "It's worth a try if your sinuses are up to it."

Austin adjusted the rearview mirror as if to check the Jeep's rear seat. Nick looked over her shoulder to see what had his interest, but there was nothing except her knapsack.

"I was wondering," he said, once he had the mirror righted again, "if that bag of yours was big enough to hold a skirt."

"I'd hate to disappoint you."

He glanced at her Levi-encased legs. "I have high hopes."

The *Courier* and its mote-filled morgue was a wasted effort. Meeks had never gone on staff, but remained a stringer from the late thirties until 1941. Probably, he'd gone into the service during World War Two, but there was no record of that.

The local phone book listed several Meekses, but no Lewis, which would have been a long shot, anyway, since he would have to be as old, or even older than Chief Tuttle.

From the Provo library, they went on-line to the Family History Library and located a death certificate for Lewis Meeks. He died in Provo on March 15, 1946. No wife or surviving children were on record.

Next, the library's database coughed up a death certificate for the state trooper, Will Jennings, who'd given Meeks his one-day exclusive on Knute and Nora's shoot-out. Both men had died the same day, March 15, 1946.

"I knew the ides of March were tough," Austin said, shaking his head, "but this is . . ." He rotated his hands to show he had no word for it.

"I don't like it either," Nick said and kept after the sluggish database, which eventually yielded the name of Trooper Jennings's surviving married daughter, Naomi Knowles, now living in Payson, Utah.

38

Harold, who'd parked across the street and half a block down from the library, blinked sweat from his eyes. A time-and-temperature sign on a nearby bank claimed 91 degrees. Harold didn't believe it. To him, the air felt combustible. Heat waves were blurring the library like a mirage, for Christ's sake. The 91 degrees had to be some kind of chamber of commerce scam.

To hell with Utah. Give him L.A. or New York anytime. He didn't give a damn about the natural wonders claimed by the guide books. You've seen one snow-covered mountain, you've seen them all. That went double for deserts.

Harold wiped the sweat from his dark glasses which, he decided, weren't dark enough for this goddamned state. Next chance he got he'd buy himself a pair of mirror lenses like the motorcycle cops.

"Shit!" Wiping his glasses had turned them into one big smear, making the miragelike heat waves even more out of focus.

A spit-cleaning didn't help. He looked up and down the street, searching for a drugstore where he could buy another pair. No luck.

He climbed out of the car, half-intending to walk to the corner to check the cross street. But he couldn't take the risk. Stretching his legs was one thing, but losing sight of his objective was quite another.

He took shade under an awning outside a one-chair barber shop. A sign next to a rotating red and white pole said, AIR CONDITIONED INSIDE. He glanced though the plate glass, where a white-smocked barber was sitting in his own chair, reading a magazine.

Harold shifted focus to the library's shimmering reflection in the plate glass and caught movement. He jerked around and realized he'd been fooled by a trick of light, sun bouncing off a passing car.

Furious for allowing himself to be distracted, Harold returned to the car, now no better than a sweatbox, and went back to doing his job, staring at the library. He counted time in his head, steeling himself against the blistering heat. He was Harold the herald, after all. Harold the messenger.

He smiled. The trick was to keep his mind busy. Heat is only an illusion, he told himself.

He snorted derisively. He'd tell that to the devil when he met him.

He closed his eyes, picturing himself in hell. His head nodded forward. The movement jerked him awake.

He grabbed a water bottle, started to pour it over his head, then decided he couldn't chance looking like a wet vagrant, and sucked it dry instead.

Focus, he told himself. In his business, daydreaming could get you killed.

Breathing deeply, he checked his rearview and side mirrors. No cops, not even a meter maid in sight. In a big city, you could time them, usually. But Provo was too small, eighty thousand the city limits sign said. Still sticksville as far as he was concerned. Too clean-cut, too sixties.

He slumped in his seat. The smaller the town, the more strangers stood out. Especially a man alone in a car.

Circle the block, instinct told him. But that was risky, if his targets chose that moment to make their move.

The cell phone rang, startling him even though it was muted. He checked the mirrors one more time before answering.

Harold crossed his fingers and said, "I'm listening."

"Where are you?"

"Still in Provo."

"I don't like your tone."

Fuck you. "Sorry, sir."

The cell phone transmitted a sound that could have been laughter. Though with a man like Fisher, Harold wouldn't have bet on it.

"We're going to try a little leverage on the Scott woman," Fisher said. "If that doesn't work . . ." He let it hang there and disconnected.

Harold expelled the breath he'd been holding, knowing that a go-order on retirement might have gotten him retired, too, especially in an uncontrolled environment like Provo. Come to think of it, the way he was sweating, they wouldn't have to retire him, he'd just melt. Melted in Utah. Christ, maybe he was already dead, and this was what hell looked like.

Salvation. The Scott woman and her friend came out of the library and headed for their car. He could run the air conditioning.

39

Payson, Utah, with its Victorian houses and picket fences reminded Nick of a moment in time captured by Norman Rockwell. Naomi Knowles lived in a gabled two-story with gingerbread eaves.

"She may not thank us for digging up the past," Austin warned as they left the Jeep and headed for the house.

"Her father died in 1946," Nick reminded him. "That's too long to grieve."

Which made Naomi Knowles seventy if she was a day, Nick decided the moment the woman opened the screen door and squinted at them from under a gnarled hand shading her eyes.

Nick introduced herself and Austin and explained their mission, to research the last days of Knute and Nora, and anyone who'd been there when the pair were shot.

"That's the last thing I would have expected on seeing you two come up the walk."

She ushered them inside. The small living room felt cool, kept that way by brick walls thick enough to create deep window sills. Naomi pointed to a narrow needlepoint loveseat. Nick and Austin sat squashed side by side as Naomi took a pink velvet Victorian wingback for herself. Had Nick uncovered the room during a dig, she would have dated the furniture from the same period as the house itself, mid-1890s.

"I was sixteen years old the day my father died," Naomi began. "It's not something you forget, even after all this time. He died on my birthday."

Her nod pointed to an oval-framed photograph of a man in uniform, colored-after-the-fact Nick guessed. Beside it hung a matching frame with a colored likeness of a woman the same age, mid-thirties.

"My parents," Naomi said. "My father kept that uniform even after they fired him from the state police. He kept it in the trunk of his Plymouth. It was still there when he was found dead beside his car, shot to death."

Nick nudged Austin's knee. She hadn't expected another violent death.

Naomi went on. "I remember them telling my mother that they'd never give up on his killer, him being an ex-officer and all. But I could hear the doubt in their voices and I was right. They never did catch anyone. At the time, they figured it was a lunatic, or maybe someone he once arrested. We'll never know for sure now."

She stared at Nick intently. "Or will we?"

"As I told you, we're archaeologists researching Utah's famous bank robbers."

Naomi nodded. "My father was there when Knute and Nora were shot, you know, at Green River."

"That's why we're here, Mrs. Knowles," Austin said. "We thought he might have told you what happened. That was April nineteen forty. You were then . . ."

"Ten years old," she supplied, then smiled. "He didn't tell about it outright. I was too young to hear such things, but I crept downstairs to listen while he told my mother all about it.

She was scared out of her wits when she heard about the shoot-out on the radio."

Naomi rose from her chair and crossed the room to stand in front of her father's photograph. Austin leaned forward as if intending to speak, but Nick silenced him with another nudge.

After a while Naomi sidestepped to her mother's photograph and said, "My father took to drink, you know, and my mother was never the same. After he was found dead, she stopped trusting people. She never did forgive my father's brother officers. She said they ought to be ashamed of themselves, not being able to find his killer. Every night, as part of our prayers, Mother used to say, if the police don't take care of their own, who will? Thinking back on it, I figure they didn't try too hard, him being a drunk and all."

Naomi gently caressed the glass covering her mother's likeness. "After a while she started thinking people were following her. When I asked who, she'd say, 'Better you don't know, daughter, otherwise they'll start following you.' Finally, she said we shouldn't talk to anyone about what happened."

Shaking her head slowly, Naomi returned to her wingback. "Mother made me swear to keep quiet and never say a word, and yet here I am talking to you."

Nick was about to offer assurances, when Naomi shook her head. "Don't worry, I don't mind telling you these things. You see, nobody ever asked me before and, well, Mother's been gone so long who could possibly care? Besides, I don't really know anything, not for sure, except what I overheard that night and what Mother told me years later. By then, she might have been a little touched, talking to my dead father the way she did."

Naomi smiled. "Come to think about it, she was my age when that started. Now, here I am, often as not talking to her while I do my housework. Maybe it runs in the family, or maybe it's just old age. Anyway, that night I crept downstairs and I heard my father say, 'It wasn't right, what happened at Green River. They didn't have to be killed.' "

"Who?" Nick asked.

"I took him to mean Knute and Nora."

"Your father lived another six years after that shooting,"

Austin reminded the woman. "He must have told you something in that time."

"I'm getting to it, young man. I heard him talking to another trooper once. They were out back, sneaking a cigarette since my mother didn't allow smoking in the house. I was under the screen porch playing with my kittens and that's when I heard it. 'Knute and Nora were trying to surrender when they were shot,' my father said. 'Something's not right.' "

She nodded as if responding to something only she could hear. "It's funny. You being here jogged my memory. A private detective came around once asking the same kind of questions."

"I thought you said no one ever asked you about Knute and Nora before?"

"I told the truth. The detective wasn't talking to me, he was talking to my mother. He came to the house at dinner time, which upset my mother because she didn't like her food getting cold, not after she'd gone to all the work of cooking it. We lived in Salt Lake in those days, so she told the detective where he could find my father. He worked at a bar out by the airport."

"And this happened when you were ten," Austin said, "right after the shooting?"

"No. It was after the war. Maybe nineteen forty-five or -six. I remember my father got mad at Mother for talking to the detective. He started shouting and swearing. When language got bad my mother always sent me to my room because young unmarried women weren't supposed to hear such things. So I couldn't have been a child anymore." She smiled at the memory. "My mother didn't start calling me a young woman until I was fifteen, the same age she got married."

Nick asked, "Do you remember the detective's name?"

"Sorry. I don't know if I ever heard it, but my father would have been able to tell you. He was a scrupulous man when it came to anything connected with his police work. He always kept a notebook."

"He wasn't a policeman anymore," Nick reminded her.

"It didn't make any difference, even when he was drinking. He'd write things down. 'You never know when you might need to jog your memory for testifying in court,' he'd say. I never saw him without one of those notebooks in his pocket."

Naomi glanced at her father's photo as if seeking approval for what she'd just said. "I stand corrected. After he was shot, when they brought home his personal belongings, his notebook was missing. Mother asked about it specially, but they told her that they'd hadn't found it on his body. His wallet was there though, with money in it." She nodded at the memory. "My mother kept the rest of father's notebooks. 'Her treasures,' she called them and locked them up in her trunk and hid them away. 'They'd be too painful to read now,' she told me at the funeral. 'Time will heal us.' But it never did, not my mother. She never looked at them again."

Naomi shrugged. "And neither have I, though maybe someday I will. I don't have any children, so nobody else is interested. They're in my mother's trunk in the fruit cellar, if the mice haven't eaten them." She pointed at the floor. "It's been sitting down there for nearly fifty years. Even my late husband, God rest him, never had a look."

Naomi wrapped her arms around herself as if the thought chilled her. "Mother used to spend all summer putting up fruit so we'd have it in the winter. Some of it's still down there, too, along with the spiders and God knows what else."

Nick leaned forward and said softly, "It would be a great help to us if we could see those notebooks."

For a moment Nick thought the woman was going to refuse, then she sighed, stood, and led them through the kitchen and out onto the back porch.

"That's the fruit cellar, right there." She pointed to a ground-level door built into the side of the house at a forty-five-degree angle. "When you finish, you'd better come back in through the kitchen so you can wash your hands." She eyed Nick's red curls. "Make sure you don't get any black widows in your hair."

Nodding, Nick drew her Cubs cap from the back pocket of her jeans and pulled it on tightly.

"I don't have a hat," Austin said.

Naomi shrugged. "There's a light switch at the bottom of the stairs." She retreated inside.

"Be my guest," Austin said, standing aside to let Nick go first.

"Arachnophobic, are we?"

Austin's answering smile looked forced.

The fruit cellar was a cement-lined pit about twelve feet square. Cobweb-covered shelves, some still brimming with canned goods, lined three sides of the pit. The other side held a furnace and a water heater. The trunk—metal, thank God, and relatively impervious to rot—stood at the end of a narrow, claustrophobic aisle leading to the furnace.

Nick cleared a path through the spider webs to reach the trunk, which she tapped with her foot to shoo off any life-forms. When nothing moved she nudged it hard enough to raise dust, but the trunk, which was about three feet long and two feet deep, didn't budge. She grabbed hold and pulled, moving it only inches.

"It feels like it's full of bricks," she told Austin over her shoulder. "I'm going to need your help dragging it back to the stairs. Once we get it there, we'll have someplace to sit while we sort through it."

Austin stopped brushing himself to peer up at the rafters close above his head.

"I don't see any spiders," Nick assured him.

Even so, he scrunched his shoulders as if the thought made him itch.

"For heaven's sake," Nick said, "turn around and let me look you over."

He pivoted slowly.

"Not a bug in sight, now give me a hand."

A thick layer of dust, undisturbed except for Nick's handprints, covered the trunk. Austin sneezed just looking at it.

"Some archaeologist. You should have gone into another line of work."

"Digging in dirt isn't the same."

"It was dusty in the caves in Boyle's Twist."

"That's different. Anasazi dust is a thousand years old. I'm not allergic to that."

"You and my father make a perfect pair."

"Thank you."

"That wasn't a compliment."

Austin ran a hand over his head, as if checking his hair for spiders one last time, then grabbed hold of the metal trunk and dragged it, screeching, across the concrete floor.

She shook her head at him. She'd asked for his help, but instead he'd risked a hernia playing macho man.

Nick collapsed onto the stairs facing the trunk. The treads weren't wide enough for the two of them to sit side by side, so Austin climbed far enough to perch behind her, where he could watch over her shoulder.

She used her cap to slap at the dust. The trunk's metal surface was badly rusted and corroding at the corners. Its spring-lock came loose at a touch. Not a good sign. Wood rot, her original fear, might have been preferable.

Mentally crossing her fingers, she opened the lid. The smell of mold was like a hand clenching her throat. That and the rancid stink of mice droppings.

Inside, paper had been shredded into nests.

She raised both her legs and kicked the trunk viciously. Nothing scurried, nothing moved.

"How do you feel about mice?" she asked over her shoulder.

"They bite," Austin answered.

Nick, who was breathing through her mouth to keep her nose at bay, nodded. "There are gloves in the Jeep."

"I'll get them."

When Austin got back, he did the honors and began rooting in the trunk one handed, trying to hold his breath as he worked. Beneath the shredded paper were stacked magazines, more or less intact, which accounted for the trunk's weight.

"I've got something," he said and sneezed. "It's on the bottom." He turned his head, gulped a breath, and plunged in both arms to the elbows.

Out came an oilcloth bundle, bound with twine. The twine burst at the first tug, but the cloth was intact. Nick reached around Austin to lower the trunk lid so they could use it as a tabletop.

Inside the oilcloth was a tin box, this one as good as new. Its hinges didn't so much as squeak when Austin opened it.

Stacked in neat rows were the notebooks of State Trooper Will Jennings. Each notebook was dated, some covering two months, others three.

Nick started with 1940 and went directly to April. There were daily entries, often several to a page, with some as terse as *Nothing to report*.

When she found the shoot-out, Jennings had expanded his initial entry. *They came out of the car with their hands up*, he wrote. *They weren't armed. Through the open door I could see Nora's machine gun on the seat, but no sign of Knute's .45. Someone yelled shoot. Everyone fired. It was a massacre. They deserved it, everyone said afterward.*

She read it to Austin who said, "We knew that already. Try the next page."

Nick went through the following three weeks but found no more references to Knute and Nora. They divided up the rest of 1940. As Jennings became more experienced, the length of his entries expanded and his observations became more detailed.

Then, in 1941, he was fired from the state police. After that, his writing began rambling and, often as not, verged on incoherence. As the years passed, daily entries gave way to weekly entries until finally they were even more sporadic.

The last notebook was dated 1945. The entries stopped after a few pages.

"Eureka!" Nick said, holding it up like a prize. " 'Knute and Nora keep coming back to haunt me,' " she read. " 'I should have told the truth when the private detective called me. He said he represented Nora's mother. He even sent me his card, asking me to call if I changed my mind.' "

Jennings had made a hand-sketched replica of the man's business card. *Decker's Detective Agency. Lamar Decker, President. We specialize in divorces.*

40

Lamar Decker stood in darkness, staring down at the street. The man in brown was still there, still watching. And Decker's office had been searched, a very professional job with nothing left out of place, not by much anyway. But enough to make Decker know he'd been had.

He paced in frustration. He'd first caught sight of the man the day before, but the bastard could have been on his tail for days, weeks even, dogging Decker's footsteps.

At first Decker had figured that his wife, Doris, was having him followed. But why would she bother? The divorce was all but final. The witch had bled him dry.

That left Irma Slater. Nothing else was pending. But that didn't make sense either. So what if Jennings had told him a surprising story. Who would believe the word of a disgruntled drunk? There were always discrepancies. People's memories couldn't be trusted any more than their eyesight.

Hell, it was ancient history, anyway. Besides, what difference did it make if Knute and Nora had been shot with their hands up? The police got itchy trigger fingers when it came to cop killers, and who could blame them?

He leaned his forehead against the window pane. The man in brown, vivid in reflected light from the café downstairs, stared up at him from across the street.

The trouble was Knute and Nora's killing spree didn't match the rest of their short-lived career, not as reported in the newspapers. Time and again, they'd boasted that they'd never stolen from the poor or killed an innocent man.

Decker grimaced. Maybe Knute and Nora didn't count cops as innocent.

He pulled back from the window and muttered, "to hell with you," at the brown man. Maybes didn't matter. None of it mattered. It was old news, over and done with.

So what the hell was the brown man up to?

A relative of one of the dead cops, maybe, who got word that Decker was snooping around.

That made sense.

He started to nod, then caught himself. If that was the case why didn't he come up to the office and tell Decker to lay off. Or threaten him, even. That Decker could understand. But just standing there, staring up at the office and watching, that was getting on Decker's nerves.

Decker went back to pacing. Maybe the brown man was after someone who worked in the café. Maybe . . .

To hell with the brown man. Decker had a meeting with Irma Slater in two days. He'd keep working on her case until then, though it sure as hell seemed like a waste of time.

He drew the blind and returned to his desk. No use taking any chances, he told himself as he assembled the notes he'd been making on the Slater case and sealed them in an envelope. He addressed it, added a stamp, and then slipped downstairs and out of the building through the basement. Once assured that the brown man was still on the other side of the street, Decker hurried to the corner and smiled to himself as he fed the envelope into the mailbox. Probably he was being paranoid, but why take a chance? He'd send his case notes to the one place no one would ever think to look.

Whistling, he strolled back to his office, climbed the stairs to the landing, and was about to open the door when he heard movement behind him. Before he could turn, a rope looped over his head and around his neck. He caught a glimpse of a brown sleeve and opened his mouth to shout but the rope cinched tight.

He reached back, flailing frantically, but he couldn't reach the man.

His feet were kicked out from under him. He fell headfirst, the brown man on top of him, his knees in Decker's back for leverage. The rope jerked, cutting into Decker's throat like wire.

Decker tried kicking but his strength was gone. His feet drummed. His last thought was of Irma Slater. He hoped she wouldn't die the same way.

Irma Slater, exhausted from the long bus ride home from Salt Lake's Federal Heights, where she cleaned houses for the rich, had just eased her swollen feet into a pan of hot water when the doorbell rang.

She sighed and called out, "Coming."

She slipped her wet feet into slippers, buttoned her housedress, and picked up the pan. Then she shuffled to the door and opened it.

The man standing under the porch light, smiling, was dressed all in brown.

4 1

Nick began the next day's research the easy way, by checking the phone books. But there was no listing for Decker's Detective Agency in Provo, Salt Lake, or Payson, and no listing for a Lamar Decker, either. Nothing even close.

"He'd be eighty by now, like everybody connected with this," Austin reminded her softly, honoring the genealogy library's quiet policy. "Maybe more, depending on how old he was at the time."

"We got lucky with Chief Tuttle, didn't we?"

Austin shrugged. They'd been first in line when the genealogy library opened that morning and were now seated side by side, facing matching computers. Austin's status as a professor at the university had gotten them a two-man cubicle to themselves.

"I'll try death notices." Nick made the entry.

Decker's date of death, March 16, 1946, stunned her. "Damn near everyone connected with Knute and Nora died in the same week," Nick whispered, then emphasized her point with a gentle jab of her elbow into Austin's ribs. "That's stretching the laws of coincidence."

Nick's heart pounded at the discovery as she checked the neighboring cubicles, but the adjacent researchers seemed unaware of her rising blood pressure. On the plus side, no one looked remotely like FBI.

She forced herself to breathe deeply. Her hands, which had dropped to her lap, seemed steady enough, though somehow she'd expected them to be shaking. The words serial killer were on the tip of her tongue, when she caught herself. *You're overreacting*. This was all ancient history, sixty years ancient. Even if a killer obsessed with Knute and Nora had been on a rampage back in 1946, he'd be an old man by now. Or woman. And statistically more likely dead than alive.

Nick leaned close to Austin. "Remember what Trooper Jennings said?"

He nodded.

She reminded him anyway. "He said, 'Something's not right.' "

"We only have his daughter's memory of that."

Nick glared at him. "All right, I'm saying it again. Something is very damned fishy."

"Don't get paranoid on me."

"Me, paranoid? You should have met . . ." She'd been about to say, my mother, but suppressed the urge. She didn't know Austin well enough to share family skeletons.

"I'm listening," Austin said.

All Nick said was, "You know I'm right about this."

"It doesn't matter if you are. Too much time's passed. Worrying about it now isn't going to change anything."

Grumbling, Nick went back to the computer. A single typed word, *strangulation*, leaped out at her from Decker's death certificate.

She tapped her blunt nail against the computer screen. "You were saying."

"Murder?"

"Unless he hanged himself, and in that case it would say suicide."

"It's still old news."

"Then why is the FBI following us?"

"You're imagining things. Nobody's been following us since we left the desert."

She shook her head. "One of them's been with us since the mountains. That, I'm sure of."

Austin looked over his shoulder.

"Don't bother," she told him. "I haven't seen him this morning."

Her cell phone's nearly silent buzz sent her outside to answer the call.

"It's me," Elliot announced. "I'm on my way to Baptist Wash."

Nick relayed the information to Austin, who was standing beside her on the sidewalk in front of the Family History Library. The 10:15 A.M. temperature was 88.

Austin shouted toward the phone, "What the hell's going on?" His comment drew nasty looks from passersby on their way to the temple across the street.

"Hold on," Nick told her father, "while we find ourselves a little privacy."

As soon as they settled into the Jeep Cherokee, Nick started the engine and switched on the air conditioner, whose hot air smelled like wet dog fur.

"Go ahead, Dad." She angled the phone so Austin could listen in by pressing himself within an inch of her cheek.

"I'm on the road right now," Elliot said. "I figure to reach Baptist Wash in four hours. Knowing the way you drive, Nick, that gives you plenty of time to meet me there."

"I thought you said the university had forbidden you?"

"So the university says."

Nick didn't like the sound of that. Her father was an institution at the University of New Mexico. Not only was he head of the department, but had an Anasazi museum named after him. Getting himself fired for insubordination would change all that.

She said, "You told me you were going to pull some strings. Is that why you're on the move?"

"I pulled them, all right." His snort sounded like static. "Jerked is more like it. Whether anyone felt the tug, it's too early to say."

"But—"

"I'm not waiting for a bunch of bureaucrats to tell me what to do," Elliot snapped, "not with those caves in Boyle's Twist waiting. Austin, are you listening to me?"

"I'm here."

"Then get your butt in gear and head south."

"If I do that, I get fired. I don't have your kind of tenure, or political pull."

"Bullshit. Once we publish those petroglyphs, universities will be standing in line to hire the both of us."

Nick shook her head, not buying it. "What about your museum, Elliot? You won't be able to take it with you."

"We'll see about that."

Nick sighed.

Elliot said, "Well, Austin, I'm waiting. Make up your mind, or Nick will leave you behind."

"Are you sure I'm coming?" she said.

"You're unemployed, daughter, so what have you got to lose?"

"Give me the phone," Austin said.

When she handed it over, he kissed her softly on the lips, then pulled away while she was still considering her response.

"Elliot," Austin said, smiling at Nick, "don't start without us." He motioned at Nick to drive the car. "We're leaving now. We should be in Baptist Wash by the time you get there."

Nick checked both mirrors for any sign of the man she thought was following them. Coming up empty, she pulled away from the curb.

"Turn right at the corner," Austin told her. "We'll pick up the freeway west of town."

Nick made the turn while Austin continued his conversation with Elliot. "We're going to be trespassing on government land." He listened a moment. "Your father says red tape be damned. We'll be in and out, photographing everything, before they know we're there. Besides, your father says the worst they can do is arrest us."

"Tell my father about all the deaths we've discovered."

Austin passed on their discoveries while Nick played dodge-'em with an eighteen-wheeler bent on denying her the merge lane. Through it all Austin's voice remained dead calm, despite his panicked gesturing at the traffic surrounding them. Once clear of the eighteen-wheeler, whose air-horn continued to blow angrily, Nick moved left to the fast lane and pushed the speed limit.

Behind them, the car Nick had been seeing since Kamas, darted out from behind the eighteen-wheeler as if to sneak a look, then disappeared behind the behemoth truck just as quickly.

Austin touched her arm with the cell phone. "He wants to speak with you, Nick."

At this speed, she needed both hands on the wheel. "Hold the phone to my ear."

Austin complied, momentarily stroking her cheek as he did so, whether by accident she couldn't be certain. The smell of his lime aftershave tickled her nose.

"Remember the prime rule of archaeology," Elliot told her. "Digging up the recent past is grave robbing. The Anasazi are safe because they don't have relatives left who can sue."

"We'll film your petroglyphs," Nick told him. "I'll even climb for you, if I have to. But after that, I'm expecting you to help with Knute and Nora."

"Can Austin hear me?"

"If he were any closer we'd be arrested."

"Keep a close eye on my daughter," Elliot counseled. "She's as stubborn as her mother."

Nick shot back, "What's that supposed to mean?"

But Elliot had already hung up.

After a moment, Austin said, "We're better off sticking to the Anasazi."

"Not just yet," she said and swerved across three lanes of fast traffic and down the exit ramp.

"What the hell are you doing?" Austin shouted.

"I wanted to make sure we aren't being followed."

"And?"

"We aren't now."

"Then get back on the freeway."

"I wasn't finished at the library. Besides, Elliot's not going to make those climbs without us."

"You know something, Nick. Stubborn doesn't begin to cover it."

4₂

This time Nick abandoned computers to rummage through the library's collection of Polk's Salt Lake City Directories, a detective's friend if she'd ever seen one. Every business in town was listed, year by year. Even the occupants of office buildings were catalogued by floor and office number. Each apartment house tenant was listed. The same went for duplexes. There was no escaping the Polk.

The 1946 edition gave Decker Detective Agency's address as 134 East Third South. His home address was also noted, 854 Third Avenue. Neither address was repeated in Polk's 1947.

She went back to the computers and called up obits on file. Lamar Decker had only one listed survivor, his ex-wife Doris Decker Tempest.

"Not much of a life," Austin said as he read the obit over Nick's shoulder, his lime aftershave once again thrilling her nose, "when all you leave behind is an ex-wife who probably hates your guts."

Nose tingling, Nick checked this year's on-line phone book for Salt Lake. At the sight of Doris Tempest, Nick crossed her fingers and said, "Maybe we just got lucky."

"The wife of a long-dead private eye. What the hell is she going to tell us?"

"Her address is on the way out of town."

Austin scowled. "How do you know that, this is my town?"

"All right, where is Canyon View Drive?"

Austin sighed. "On the way out of town."

"You see," Nick said triumphantly, "my luck's changing already."

On the phone, Doris Tempest had told Nick she couldn't miss the house. It was the only Cape Cod on the block.

Nick drove right past it, before Austin caught the mistake. The Tempest home had gray brick instead of clapboard siding, aluminum shutters, and dormers like bleak afterthoughts.

Doris Tempest stepped out to meet them on the concrete porch. Her blue eyes twinkled behind rimless glasses that had slipped halfway down her nose. She looked to be in her eighties, white-haired, with a trim figure despite a billowing, brightly flowered smock.

"We can sit out here if you like," Mrs. Tempest said once introductions were made. "But it's cooler inside."

Inside, blinds had been drawn against the sun, whose glow washed the small living room with yellow light. Nick waited for guidance about seating. Mrs. Tempest smiled at the courtesy and pointed Nick to a reclining chair facing the sofa. Skid marks on the carpet showed that the chair had been turned away from the TV set for the occasion.

Mrs. Tempest took one end of the sofa, which left Austin the other end. At her elbow, a glass-topped end table held a hinged, double-sided silver frame containing two photographs of what appeared to be the same man, one version young, the other gray-haired and distinguished looking.

"Now, dear," Mrs. Tempest said, "you told me on the

phone you were an archaeologist looking into something that might involve my first husband." Her encouraging nod dislodged her glasses farther down her nose. "I don't think Lamar would have known what an archaeologist is."

Briefly, Nick related her discovery of Knute and Nora's Packard and her desire to document the last days of the notorious pair.

Mrs. Tempest shook her head. "I never heard Lamar mention Knute and Nora. That I would have remembered."

"As far as we can tell your husband was asking questions about the day Knute and Nora died. Do you have any idea why he would have done that, or who might have hired him to do so?"

Mrs. Tempest studied Nick over the top of her glasses. "When was that exactly?"

"They were shot in April 1940, trying to make their getaway at the Green River crossing."

"I can't help you. I hadn't met Lamar by then. I was still in high school."

Nick recalculated her estimate of the woman's age, mid-seventies at least. "When did you meet him?"

"During the war, here in Salt Lake. My first job was driving a bus, if you can believe it. Wartime changed everything. Women had to pitch in while the men were away fighting."

"And your husband?"

"My ex, you mean. He was too old to be drafted, just barely. That's why I ended up marrying him, because there wasn't much else to choose from. A big mistake of course."

"What kind of man was he?"

"Good looking, I'll give him that. But a womanizer. Strange when you think about it, because that was his job, catching other men cheating on their wives. He should have known better."

Mrs. Tempest pursed her lips as if condemning herself. "He'd take pictures of cheating husbands, blow them up into nasty looking black-and-whites, and then lend a sympathetic shoulder for all those betrayed women to cry on. Half the time they'd end up in bed with Lamar, maybe to spite their husbands or maybe just to prove they still had sex appeal. When I found out he was cheating on me, I hired one of Lamar's rivals to get me some of those nasty pictures. They were dandies, too."

Smiling at the memory, Mrs. Tempest adjusted her glasses back to the bridge of her nose. "After that, Lamar started following me around, trying to catch me at it like all those ladies who'd come to him. But I knew him too well to get caught."

The glint in her eye made Nick think Mrs. Tempest hadn't been faithful, only careful.

"It was a bitter divorce, but I cleaned him out in the end, not that there was much to get. It was the alimony that stuck in Lamar's craw. He got so far behind, I had to sue him. I never did get much out of him, though. First, he never made much of a living as a detective, and then he got himself killed."

"I'm sorry," Nick said, though it seemed a useless comment after so many years.

"Don't be. Lamar left me his insurance, named me his beneficiary. You could have knocked me over with a feather when the check arrived. It more than made up for all that lost alimony."

"He loved you after all, then."

Mrs. Tempest shrugged. "Maybe he forgot to change his insurance policy after we got divorced. Still, I'm willing to give him the benefit of the doubt."

From his end of the sofa, Austin raised an eyebrow and pointedly looked at his watch, reminding her that they had a long drive ahead of them to Baptist Wash.

"Where are my manners?" Mrs. Tempest said suddenly. "In this kind of weather there's nothing like lemonade to beat the heat. I'll be right back."

She disappeared through an archway into the kitchen, returning almost immediately with a tray holding a green, Depression glass pitcher and three matching glasses. That particular color, Nick knew, turned the glass slightly radioactive.

"There now," Mrs. Tempest said as she filled the green glasses, "this will quench your thirst."

As Nick drank, she reminded herself that radioactivity didn't leach into lemonade, even lemonade so tart it puckered her mouth.

Mrs. Tempest nodded at Nick's surprised expression. "Nature's way is best, dear. Sugar just makes you more thirsty."

Nick forced herself to keep drinking. Austin went along.

"Now, where were we?" Mrs. Tempest asked.

Austin spoke up. "We have reason to believe that your husband was hired by Nora Deacons's mother to look into the shooting at Green River."

Mrs. Tempest raised an eyebrow. "What does 'reason to believe' mean?"

"We have a statement from a state trooper your husband questioned," Nick explained, embellishing on the handwritten note Will Jennings had left behind.

"I never had anything to do with my husband's business," Mrs. Tempest said. "We didn't talk about it, either, so I never knew what he was up to."

She refilled Nick's glass, then hovered beside Austin until he emptied his glass enough to be topped off. Once seated again on the sofa she said, "Why is all this so important to you after all this time?"

Nick looked to Austin, whose expression left the dirty work to her. Probably he didn't believe in Nick's theory of multiple murder. She wasn't all that sure she believed it herself. What the hell. The worst the woman could do was laugh in her face.

"Mrs. Tempest," Nick began, choosing her words carefully, "three people connected with Knute and Nora died in the same week. A state trooper who witnessed the shoot-out, Irma Slater, Nora's mother, and your husband. Your husband's death certificate lists cause of death as strangulation."

"He was murdered, if that's what you're asking, and whoever did it never got caught. Maybe it was my fault, maybe I should have turned Lamar's file over to the police sooner. But it didn't seem important at the time."

Nick and Austin spoke in unison. "What file?"

"The one Lamar mailed to me just before he died. By the time I received it, he was dead. Why he sent it to me, I don't know. We hadn't spoken a word to each other in a year. The fact is, when it arrived I thought maybe he'd done the right thing, finally, and sent me an alimony check."

"Maybe that's why he sent it," Nick said, "because nobody would expect it."

"That's what I figured when I opened it. 'Doris,' I said to myself, 'he had to be desperate to send it to you.' "

"But you did show it to the police eventually?"

Mrs. Tempest shrugged. "No. It didn't seem to have any connection with his death. I mean, it wasn't going to bring him back, was it?"

"Did anyone else come looking for it?" Austin asked.

"No. I'd changed my name by then, of course. It was just a single page letter, anyway. I keep it right here with his photograph." She leaned forward far enough to retrieve the hinged silver frame on the coffee table. "These are my two husbands. Since they've both passed on, I figured they wouldn't mind standing side by side. The young one's Lamar."

"They look very much alike," Nick said.

Mrs. Tempest smiled. "I guess that says something about me, doesn't it." She fussed with the frame for a moment, loosening the backing far enough to slide out a plastic sleeve containing the letter, which she handed to Nick.

Nick wiped her hands on her jeans before pinching open the sleeve and extracting the fragile paper, a single sheet typewritten on Decker's letterhead.

Interview with former Utah State Trooper Will Jennings, March 14, 1946. Subject said that he was present when Knute and Nora Deacons tried to surrender after driving through a roadblock at Green River, Utah. They came out of their car with their hands raised, subject said. Subject said they weren't armed and that Knute yelled, "We give up." That's when the FBI gave the order to fire. The order came from the head of the FBI, J. Edgar Hoover, subject said. Subject also said, the FBI had been tipped off about the Green River location by a woman informant, who was there at Green River. Subject said he saw Hoover give the reward money to the woman himself. So far, I have been unable to confirm any of this.

43

Back in the Jeep, with a handwritten copy of Decker's report added to her file, Nick excitedly thrust out her hand for a congratulatory high-five. Austin parlayed it into a hug. When the hug progressed to a kiss, she shook free. If Austin continued to behave like this he was going to become an encumbrance.

"Now we know why the FBI's raising hell," she said, trying to divert him. "They're protecting their patron saint, J. Edgar."

Austin licked his lips as if savoring her taste. "From what, bad publicity fifty years after the fact?"

"After Waco and Ruby Ridge, why not?"

"We can't prove Hoover was there."

"You're forgetting that old photo at the Historical Society. We get that enhanced and we're in business."

"Maybe," he said.

"Whose side are you on?"

"The Anasazi."

"You're starting to sound like Elliot."

"I could do worse."

"You could at that." She started the engine, shifted into gear, and then switched off. "You'd better drive, I'm too wound up."

Austin beckoned her out of the driver's seat, preparing to switch places.

"Wouldn't it be easier to go around?"

"Where's the fun in that?"

"We're not here to have fun."

"Have it your way," he sulkily replied.

After they had changed places, Nick said curtly, "Now drive. Otherwise, Elliot will have the Anasazi all to himself."

"That's not all he'll have to himself," Austin muttered.

The moment they were underway, she started sorting through her file. The FBI's informant, referred to in Decker's report, confirmed the IOU Hyrum Boyle had left behind for Knute Deacons, the one saying he hadn't taken a penny of his wife's reward money.

She relayed the confirmation to Austin.

"Don't tell me," he said, "you want me to turn around and drive back to the genealogy library."

"My guess is she's got to be as dead as everybody else connected with this. She'd have to be a hundred, anyway."

"Where does that leave us, then?"

"Us? I thought your only interest was in the Anasazi."

"Besides you, you mean?"

Nick liked the sound of that, but kept it to herself. He glanced at her questioningly.

"Keep your eyes on the road," she told him.

"Yes, ma'am," he said cheerfully.

He was a careful driver, she noticed, sticking right to the speed limit. Had Elliot been at the wheel, heading toward a rendezvous with Anasazi petroglyphs, Nick would have had white knuckles and clenched teeth.

She leaned back, shut her eyes, and mulled over Lamar

Decker's single-page report. If J. Edgar Hoover had been there when Knute and Nora were killed, why wasn't it publicized? Certainly, the old boy loved the limelight. As far as she could see, there was only one explanation. Knute and Nora hadn't been Hoover's target. He was after the documents. And apparently, the only reason he hadn't found them was that Knute and Nora had left them behind in Baptist Wash.

If her reasoning was correct, if Hoover had been after the documents, he'd been protecting the president. The question was how far had he gone? Getting rid of the witnesses was one way to do it, but why wait until 1946?

Nick snapped her fingers. *Because that's when Decker had been hired to look into Knute and Nora's deaths.*

Nick shared her thoughts with Austin.

"You're saying that Hoover had them killed? You can't be serious."

"They're dead, aren't they?"

"The detective was murdered, I admit that. But detectives do sleazy work and make enemies."

"And the state trooper?"

"You've got me, there. The why still escapes me."

"It has to be those documents," she said.

"You said yourself, they could be fake."

"It doesn't make any difference. Either way, they could have been used to blackmail FDR. That or discredit him."

"You're guessing?"

"Why else would the FBI still be involved?"

"After all this time?"

"Well, maybe it's still going on. Maybe Hoover put a kind of inner circle together that the rest of the FBI doesn't know about. A kind of dirty tricks department that's still active."

Austin's fingers drummed on the steering wheel until he said finally, "Okay, so I can't think of another good explanation."

He pulled over to the shoulder of the road and grabbed his cell phone. "I've got to call the university and let them know I'll be out of town. Otherwise, I'm out of a job for sure." He punched a preprogrammed number.

"Fisher, this is Dr. Austin. I'll be in southern Utah for the next day or two."

44

Harold drank the last of Mrs. Tempest's lemonade and smacked his lips dramatically. "That's the best I've ever had. Too many people kill the taste with sugar."

Mrs. Tempest beamed.

Harold beamed back, secure in the knowledge that she'd swallowed his line and thought that his phony FBI credentials were the real thing. "I want to thank you for sharing your husband's letter with me. I hope it didn't bring back too many unhappy memories."

"Like I told Miss Scott, it all happened a long time ago. And pretty soon now there won't be anybody left to remember anything. I'm no spring chicken, that's sure."

"You don't look a day over sixty," Harold lied. "You'll be telling tales for years." *Unless I have to kill you.* He crossed his fingers. *Killing a woman*

Mrs. Tempest's age would be a little like killing his own mother.

He handed back the original letter, plus an extra copy he'd made for her. "Lucky I had a copy machine in my car. Now I have one for myself and you have an extra."

"Technology's a marvel. People around here, people my age, are afraid of change, but machines can be real time-savers. Take that poor Scott woman. She had to copy it all down by hand."

"You're young at heart, just like I said."

She beamed again.

"If you'll excuse me," he added, "I have a call to make."

"You're welcome to use my phone. It's in the kitchen."

"I'm afraid it's long distance. Besides, I have a phone right in my car."

She nodded. "Another marvel. Even here in Payson, I see people talking on their telephones right out in public. Talking and driving, that's another matter. I don't hold with such things."

"I'm not going anywhere yet," he assured her.

"I'll make another pitcher of lemonade, then."

His stomach curdled at the thought as he ambled down the walk to his car. He swallowed repeatedly, trying to clear the sour taste from his mouth. Maybe the woman didn't have the money for sugar to sweeten her lemonade. He glanced back at the house. Ugly but well kept. So probably money wasn't a factor. He shrugged. Women's motives eluded him.

His encrypted call was answered immediately. He read Fisher the letter word for word.

"Read it again," Fisher commanded.

When Harold finished the second time there was silence on the line except for a faint electronic hum. Harold pressed the phone hard against his ear and waited.

When Fisher spoke at last, the hum disappeared. Harold listened to his orders intently.

"Do you understand?" Fisher concluded. "I want no mistakes."

"Yes, sir," Harold said and hung up. Perhaps he'd only imagined the hum. Or maybe he'd been hearing the bees humming in the flowers that lined the sidewalk leading to the door.

Inside the house again, with fresh lemonade at hand, Harold

clicked glasses with Mrs. Tempest, who sat across from him at the kitchen table, their knees almost touching.

"You're lucky to live in such a peaceful place," he said, staring out at the orchards in the distance.

Mrs. Tempest followed his gaze. "Payson's known for its fruit trees."

"It must be beautiful when they're in bloom."

"Like heaven."

He seized on the word. "You know what I do sometimes. I try to imagine heaven. I close my eyes and pretend I'm flying to heaven." He squeezed his eyes to slits to show her the way.

When she closed hers, he broke her neck. It would be easy to make it look like an accident.

45

Irma Slater didn't like the looks of the man in the brown suit one bit. "What do you want?" she called out.

"Mrs. Slater?" he asked.

"Who wants to know?" She thought the man looked insincere.

"Mr. Decker sent me. He has important news for you."

Well that accounted for it, she thought. Those private detectives were all scum of the earth. She put her pan of water down and opened the door. "You'd best come in," she said.

She turned her back and picked up the pan, regretting the hot, soothing soak she had planned. She had no more than shuffled forward a few feet when she felt the biting pain of something around her neck. It was purely a reflex action that made her fling the hot water backward. The water wasn't scalding, but it made the man loosen his grip for an instant. That was enough.

Irma Slater had earned her living all her life through manual labor. She was a strong woman and she was fighting for her life. She brought the pan down hard on the man's head and then broke away. She hadn't taken two steps and the man was on her again. But those two steps were enough. Her heavy hot iron sitting on the ironing board in the kitchen was within reach. She grabbed it and swung with all her might. There was a sickening crunch of bone and it was all over. The man lay crumpled at her feet.

"God have mercy on me," Irma cried and started to shake. Whatever was she going to do. She fumbled through her things and found Lamar Decker's card. With trembling fingers she dialed his number. There was no answer.

It was late. There was no reason for him to be at his office. But the man had said he'd come from Decker. What should she do? She took a deep breath to steady her nerves. She and her daughter Nora were not so very different in temperament. They could keep their heads when the chips were down.

Irma took all the money she had in the house and threw it into her purse. She left everything else behind. She'd take a bus to Decker's office. If everything looked OK she'd call the police about the dead man in her home. If she found what she was afraid she'd find, she'd just keep on going. She knew from her previous experience on the coast that the rich people in California were always looking for someone to clean their homes.

46

Paul Fisher stared out at the ugly Los Angeles sprawl, glad that smog limited visibility to half a mile. Yet even within that radius the acrid haze was thick enough to blur everything like a bad Impressionist painting. Forever out of focus and impossible to grasp, that was how he thought of L.A. Make-believe packaged to look real, courtesy of Hollywood.

He smiled at the image. He was packaging Nelson Bishop the same way, with a Hollywood spin. Wrap him in good causes and sell him to the public like a movie star. What was the presidency, after all, but a great part. Ronald Reagan said so himself. The question was, was Bishop a good enough actor? More to the point, was he an actor with guts?

God's going to get you, his mother would have said. But it wasn't God that worried Fisher, it was the thought of Washington, Lincoln, and Jefferson rolling in their graves.

He shook himself. Conscience was something made up by the pious to keep their followers in line. Nothing to do with him. Besides, he didn't have to get his hands dirty, just follow orders, assuming Bishop had the grit to give them. If called to account, Fisher would invoke the classic Nuremberg defense, unacceptable half a century ago, but acceptable these days when the buck never stopped.

So why was he having this argument with himself? Because one word from him had gotten an old woman killed. And it couldn't stop there, not now. A chain reaction was called for, just as it had been back in 1946. Strike that. It was the same chain reaction, loose ends from the 1940s coming back to haunt them. Loose ends that no one had foreseen at the time. Lamar Decker's death should have been an end to it, his and Irma Slater's.

Fisher shook his head. Whoever had been running the operation back in 1946 should have been more careful.

He paced, wondering what he would have done had he been there. Torture Decker before disposing of him, for one thing. For another, make certain all files and letters between Decker and his ex-wife had been destroyed.

Enough! he told himself. Without time travel, second guessing was fruitless. All that mattered now was closing the Spider File once and for all.

So call Harold back and give the final orders. After that, the risk would be minimal. Once Harold was eliminated, there would be no risk. Not quite nil, though. Not if the 1946 repercussions were anything to go by.

Fisher picked up the internal phone. Now was the time to come to Jesus, as they say. Time to show Nelson Bishop the videotape. Time to see if the man was presidential material.

The videotape had been transferred from a film made by Bishop's father twenty years before his death in 1980. His son, Nelson Bishop III, Three-B, had been ten years old at the time.

The senior Nelson had delivered the tape into Fisher's hands personally, along with written instructions. The tape was to be revealed to his son only if there was, as senior had put it, "life and death risk from the Spider."

Fisher repeated those instructions to the junior Nelson, whose glaring eyes flashed with anger. "I don't care what orders my father gave you, I don't like being kept in the dark, especially by someone who works for me."

"I made the same objection to your father," Fisher explained. "I said it wasn't my place. His exact words were, 'You're the only one I trust.'"

Bishop, his hostility subsiding, settled into a maroon leather armchair. "He said the same thing to me before he died. That I was to trust you. I had no choice at the time."

"And now?"

"You're here, aren't you?"

Fisher smiled. Three-B was sounding like a politician already.

Bishop swung a foot over the arm of his chair and nodded at the television screen, a signal to go ahead. Fisher triggered the remote.

Numbers flashed on the screen, leader from the original film. When the leader ran out, there was a long, establishing shot of Nelson Bishop, Jr., seated behind the same Chippendale desk still used by his son. The on-screen Bishop waited for the camera to move in before he began to speak. His voice had the same New England polish his son had acquired at prep school and later Yale.

"My son, it's time I told you about my father, your grandfather. I know you've heard the stories about him, some from me, some from your mother, not to mention the ones you've read about."

Bishop's eyed tracked with the TelePrompTer. "Shortly after the turn of the century, my century not yours, your grandfather's genius made him one of the most powerful men in the country. His only equals were men like Carnegie, Rockefeller, and Mellon, all famous names in American history. Your grandfather, however, was obsessed with privacy, unlike the celebrity rich of today. He kept his name out of the newspapers.

"This was no easy feat, since he wielded great power, greater even than his more famous counterparts like the Carnegies. 'I prefer to manipulate history from behind the scenes,' he was fond of saying. It was no idle boast either. His power to influence legislation was legendary. Senators bent their knee to him, as did presidents. So great was his reach and influence that his close friend, J. Edgar Hoover, once called him, 'America's invisible spider.' "

On camera, Bishop smiled. Off camera, Fisher swallowed so sharply he winced.

"Hence the name Spider File," Bishop continued. "It was opened early in 1940, at your grandfather's urging. It became a joint effort of like-minded men, Mr. Hoover among them. It contains details of our crusade to discredit the socialist, Franklin Roosevelt, and thereby derail his bid for re-election in 1940. I say *our* file because I was a young man then, still of draft age and FDR had plans to get us into a foreign war.

"Some might say time has proved him right, but Hitler could have been managed, eliminated even, but only after he'd been allowed to destroy the true threat, Communist Russia."

On camera Bishop paused to sip water from a cut-crystal glass. Hearing him now, the first time since the filming, Fisher marveled at the man's ability to dismiss treason so lightly. The thought that anyone, even the Bishops, could have managed Hitler was laughable. Then again, Fisher hadn't known Nelson Bishop, Sr., the Spider, except by reputation. A reputation that would have labeled Hitler as just another fly in the man's web.

"In any case," Bishop went on, "the Spider documents were fabricated by experts known to the FBI. They were, Hoover assured us, perfect, undetectable even by experts. He convinced us that it was merely a matter of arranging an immaculate discovery. Those were his words. That way, he said, no one could possibly suspect fraud.

"At this point I should tell you that copies of all pertinent documents are stored in our Swiss bank, should you need them. The only other copy is in the Spider File itself which, since inception, has been overseen by a succession of archivists at the FBI, none of whom ever knew its contents.

"Our plan called for the documents to be placed in a bank

run by one of the president's close friends, there to be discovered by legitimate bank examiners."

On tape, Bishop paused to shake his head. "It would have worked, too, if it hadn't been for a pair of bank robbers. When news came of their robbery, your grandfather turned to Hoover and said, 'I'll see you dead if this gets out.' I'll give Hoover credit. He didn't so much as flinch. The plan could still work, he said. In fact, he thought the bank robbers might actually be a stroke of luck, that having the documents turn up in their hands would assure provenance."

Three-B jumped to his feet and shouted, "Stop the fucking tape!"

Startled, Fisher pushed the wrong button, rewind, before managing to stop the playback.

Bishop ranted, "What the hell was my father thinking about? He must have been out of his mind."

"To be fair, it was your grandfather's idea, along with Hoover and a few other like-minded men."

"Yeah, and now I'm stuck with it. Old farts thinking they know what's best for this country. Bullshit. All they cared about was their bottom lines."

"They call themselves The Eight. Not much of a name, if you ask me."

"Spare me your conspiracy theories, Fisher. The next thing you'll be telling me is they hired Lee Harvey Oswald."

"You were kept free of it deliberately. Your hands were to remain clean."

He spread his own hands, a placating gesture, but Bishop wouldn't be appeased. "I can kiss the presidency good-bye, that's for goddamn sure."

"That's why we're here, to look at our options."

"When a man like you starts mentioning options, I know I'm not going to like them."

"You don't have any choice."

"I can walk away."

Fisher wheedled, "Just hear your father out."

"I would have made a good president," Bishop said wistfully.

"You still can be."

Shaking his head, Bishop returned to his chair, leaned back against the expensive leather and said, "Just get on with it."

From the screen his father said, "Hoover ordered a massive manhunt, though he stayed carefully behind the scene. He had agents scouring the state. The longer the hunt went on, of course, the greater the risk. Then came the news that we had them, thanks to an informant. All that remained was to retrieve our documents and destroy FDR. Naturally, the robbers, Knute and Nora Deacons by name, had to be silenced. Your grandfather knew that and so did I. Hoover agreed and gave the order to have them shot. But the documents weren't on them, and our informant, a woman, didn't know their whereabouts. Neither did her husband, a simple-minded prospector.

"The plan against Roosevelt had to be suspended until the documents were recovered, which never happened, unfortunately. So, if you're seeing this, my son, it means those damned things have turned up at last.

"My advice to you, from the grave as it were, is to do anything necessary to keep the Spider File from going public. I've lived with this for years. I'd always hoped to shift the blame to Hoover should the need arise. But Hoover, being Hoover, protected himself. In the event the original documents taken by Knute and Nora go public, a second file will be activated from the FBI's archives. That file—Hoover showed it to me himself—documents our family's complete history. And I mean complete. Your grandfather could have taught Hitler tricks when it came to ruthlessness."

Onscreen, Nelson Bishop, Jr., smiled. "Mr. Fisher, if you're there as you should be, you know what to do."

The tape ran out.

"Now what?" Three-B said irritably.

Fisher, who'd been mulling over the text prepared like scripture so many years ago, wet his lips expectantly. "Your father anticipated greatness for you. You were to reap the rewards of the money that he and his father had amassed, often as not at the expense of others. But you were to be different. You were to make the Bishop name respectable at last."

Three-B raised both arms as if appealing to the gods. "All

in a day's work for us Bishops, smearing the name of one of our greatest presidents. Next, you're going to tell me they backed Hitler."

Fisher bit his tongue. Nelson Bishop, Sr., had once dined with Hitler at Berchtesgaden in the 1930s.

Fisher said, "Without Bishop money, your philanthropy wouldn't have been possible. Think of the medical research going on as we speak, or the low-cost housing projects, or scholarships—"

"Enough with the propaganda."

"Your father knew that his money would one day put the presidency within your reach."

Bishop lurched out of his chair and rapped his knuckles against the onscreen image of his father. "And now he's snatching it away."

"No, he's telling you it's time to be a realist."

"Which means?"

"You heard him. He told you to do whatever's necessary to keep the Spider File secret."

"I'm listening."

Fisher took a deep breath. "What comes next is for your eyes only."

"What the hell does that mean?"

"Men have died keeping the secret."

"How many?"

Fisher shrugged. "I was never given that information."

"So where does that leave us?"

Fisher took a sealed package from his briefcase.

"What is it?" Bishop demanded.

"Please check the seal and verify that it's intact."

Bishop grabbed it. "Okay, it's intact. Now what?"

"It's another videotape, I believe. I suggest you play it. I'll be waiting in my office."

47

Nick, half-blind from glare despite her sunglasses, rubbed her eyes at the sight of Baptist Wash. Beyond it, the Devil's Door shimmered in the heat like a mirage. But it was real enough, an enormous reef of red sandstone that marked the beginning of badlands so desolate that roads went around it. Here, the Anasazi had felt safe. Nick couldn't say the same for herself.

"Stop the car!" she snapped at Austin and released her seat belt before the Jeep rolled to a stop. They hadn't seen another vehicle since turning off Notom Road, but Nick wanted to be sure they weren't being followed.

The road behind looked clear enough. No telltale dust in the distance. Farther away, clouds shrouded the Wasatch Mountains.

"What do you think?" Nick asked

when Austin stepped out to join her. "You know this country better than I do."

The radio had been reporting showers for Hanksville and Cainville, but overhead, the sky was clear and brutal despite the sun's late afternoon descent toward night.

Austin shrugged. "It will be dark in a couple of hours, so it's too late to work Boyle's Twist today, anyway. Tomorrow maybe the forecast will have changed."

"Remember what happened in Kamas. Showers are one thing, but a cloudburst . . ." She shuddered at the thought. A gully-washer in the Wasatch, even miles away, would hit Baptist Wash like a fire hose.

Nick turned to gaze at the funnel-shaped canyon leading to the town site of Baptist Wash. The only high ground visible was the red rock barrier reef itself. "Let's see what Elliot has to say."

Elliot had already pitched camp and was drinking instant coffee and listening to his twenty-four-hour weather radio. His car, a Jeep Cherokee like Nick's, was crammed with equipment. Hers held its usual iron rations, bottled water, freeze-dried food, energy bars, and her .30-.30 rifle, plus a box of ammunition.

"You should have gotten here earlier," Elliot said the moment they were in hailing range. He was wearing his lightweight canvas fisherman's vest with pockets everywhere, some of them watertight, many bulging with site maps, energy bars, and whatever else Elliot thought necessary at the moment. "The weather might not hold."

"We've been listening," she told him.

"On the other hand, I think it's worth the risk, considering what's waiting for us in Boyle's Twist."

"Like a flash flood."

Elliot ignored her comment to focus on Austin. "What are the odds of a flood this time of year, in hundred-degree heat? Astronomical, I'd say."

Austin scuffed his toe through the bone-dry soil. "It may not look like it, but this is the rainy season. Any later in the year and it doesn't rain in those mountains, it snows. After that, it's a matter of run-off, not cloudbursts."

Impatiently, Elliot waved away the comment. "Time's a factor. To get here, you and Nick had to drive through Hanksville. For all we know the locals have alerted the FBI to our presence. Tomorrow morning may be the only chance we get."

Nick caught the twinkle in Elliot's eyes. To Austin, it would mean nothing. But she knew her father. He was testing Austin's commitment.

Nick fixed Elliot with a condemning stare she'd learned from Elaine. "You talk a good game."

"What's that supposed to mean?"

"If you don't know, I won't tell you." Another line from Elaine's repertoire of put-downs. In this case, Nick knew her father like a book. He might risk his own life for his precious Anasazi, possibly even Austin's, but never his daughter's.

Elliot tried to glare back but a smile broke through. "Okay, you win."

"Am I missing something?" Austin asked.

"You came in in the middle," Elliot told him, "so it's hard to explain."

"Try me."

Elliot shook his head. "So where do we start in the morning?"

"How about the kiva cave," Nick suggested. "In case you've forgotten, I left the rope ladder in place. I think we'll be high enough there if it floods."

Her father nodded. "Good idea. After that, I want to tackle my mystery cave." He crossed his fingers. "Weather permitting."

Nick and Austin exchanged bewildered looks before speaking at the same time. "What mystery cave?"

"I spotted it before you two got here. We missed it before. I would have missed it again if the light hadn't been just right. It's not much more than a crevice, actually."

Wind gusted, moaning in the slot canyons.

"The ghost of Baptist Boyle," Austin joked.

"Ghosts I'm not afraid of," Elliot said.

"And killers?" Nick shot back.

Elliot put an arm around her shoulders. "Stop worrying about what happened fifty years ago."

"To quote my mother, 'Old sins cast the longest shadows.' "

"She was talking about me," Elliot retorted.

48

In Los Angeles Nelson Bishop vented his rage at his father's freeze-framed video image. "You bastard! You didn't have the guts to tell me to my face, did you? Oh, no, you left a tape behind to do your dirty work. By the way, son, I'm a mass murderer. Your grandfather, too, of course. The killer Bishops, that's us."

Bishop leaned close to the television screen and spat, "Guilt isn't contagious, you old bastard. Real life isn't some Old Testament tale about the sins of the fathers being passed on to their sons."

Like hell!

Bishop rewound the videotape, the one meant for his eyes only. When the counter reached the desired point, he stopped the tape.

He took a deep breath, then another, before pressing the playback button. His father shimmied momentarily, then said, "Should you ever need to use such deadly force, don't make my mistake. I trusted the FBI and look where it got me. Got you, actually, since you're watching this tape. Take my advice. From now on trust no one but yourself. Leave no witnesses."

The tape ran out, and for a long time Bishop sat staring at the blank screen. Finally, he nodded to himself, ejected the tape from the VCR, and destroyed it, just as his father had instructed.

He stared at his hands. To be president, he would have to get them dirty. He ground his teeth. Now wasn't the time for word games. He'd have to get them bloody. The question was, did the goal justify that much blood-letting?

Certainly, he'd make a good president. Maybe even a great one. And think of how many people he could help from the Oval Office. He nodded. That wasn't a word game; it was the truth.

He picked up the direct line. When Fisher answered, Bishop said, "We'll take the corporate jet. Have your man, Harold, meet us at the Provo airport."

49

Deep inside Boyle's Twist, Nick grabbed the last handhold and pulled herself into Elliot's mystery cave. The cave's opening wasn't much wider than she was. It had been an easy climb, no more than forty feet above the canyon floor. An unlikely cave, she'd thought when he showed it to her. Too low and too small to hold Anasazi treasures. Better explored than not, Elliot had insisted. All she could see at the moment was a black hole.

They'd already rephotographed their original finds in the Kiva cave, using both conventional 35mm film and a digital camera.

Nick checked the sky, as much as she could see of it through the canyon's narrow opening a hundred and fifty feet above her. Five feet of clear blue. Her view to the west, toward the mountains, was totally obstructed.

This morning, the weather radio was predicting scattered showers only.

Nick uncoiled the rope ladder she'd wound around herself. If the cave turned out to be a dud, she'd dump it over the side rather than be burdened on the climb down. Once free of the rope, she dug into her backpack for her flashlight. And there on the wall beside her was H. BOYLE, #11. The old boy had been everywhere. No site untainted.

She leaned over the edge, cupped her hands around her mouth, and shouted, "Boyle beat us to it."

"Shit!" echoed in the canyon.

By rote, Nick followed procedure, playing her light over every inch of wall as she crawled along. Nothing showed but red rock all the way to the back of the cavern. She was about to turn back when she spotted a narrow fissure to her right. She shined her light inside. The fissure, possibly wide enough to wriggle through if you were thin enough, led to another cave. And there, caught in her beam of light, was another magnificent, though somewhat faded petroglyph, five claustrophobic feet away.

She tested the narrow opening by squeezing in an arm and a leg. She might wiggle through, barely. But Elliot and Austin wouldn't stand a chance.

The alternative was to photograph what they could see from here. Faced with such an option, she could already hear Elliot asking for volunteers to clamber through. Meaning her, the only one who could possibly fit.

She crawled back to the front of the cave, relayed her find, and began driving pitons to attach the rope ladder.

Ten minutes later Elliot and Austin took turns thrusting their heads inside the fissure to get as close a look as possible.

"It's faded. My guess is water damage," Elliot pronounced after a while.

Austin, bathed in light from their battery lanterns, nodded his agreement.

"Have you tried crawling through?" Elliot added.

"No," she told him. "As you can see, it narrows in the middle."

"Not much." Elliot looked her up and down. "Have you put on weight?"

She resisted the temptation to pat his paunch. "And if I get stuck?"

"We can always chop you out."

Elaine was right. Elliot was obsessive. The trouble was, so was she. The part that wanted to be first on the site of a new discovery was urging her to throw caution to the wind.

She was about to agree when a blast of wind, magnified by the canyon walls, howled through Boyle's Twist, and for an instant, before reason kicked in, hair prickled on the back of her neck. Red dust swirled in the cavern.

Half-blinded and coughing, Nick edged around Austin and felt her way to the front of the cave to eyeball the weather. The sky, though still blue, was tarnished by dust.

She grabbed the rope ladder with one hand, anchoring herself, and hung out precariously to get a better view toward the mountains to the west. From that angle she was able to see beyond the next switchback in the canyon and caught a glimpse of black ominous cloud.

She wet her gritty lips and shouted, "You'd better see this!"

One look and Elliot said, "We're in trouble if we don't get out of this cave."

He pointed to striations on the canyon's opposite wall, showing a history of high-water marks. Many were above the level of their perch.

"They could be hundreds of years old," Nick pointed out.

"Try nineteen eighty-seven and ninety-three," Austin said.

"Then we'd better move out," Elliot declared.

"And the petroglyph?" Nick asked.

"It's not worth the risk."

You see, Elaine, his obsession does have limits.

Nick grabbed her backpack and was about to toss it over the side when she heard a car engine. It sounded close, though that could have been an illusion, carried through the slot canyon on the wind.

"That's them," Austin said, his voice cracking.

"Who?" she asked. "The FBI?"

Austin backed against the wall and slowly sank to the ground, hugging his knees, fear in his eyes. Nick gritted her teeth, remembering the kiss in the car. She sure could pick 'em. She knelt in front of him. "What the hell have you done?"

"I told them where we were going."

"Who?"

Austin shook his head. "My grant came from the Bishop Foundation, that's who. They threatened to take it away. They might as well have taken my life. 'No grant, no book, no job,' that's what they said. It's all your fault. If you hadn't used the Internet to get information their scanning programs would never have been alerted. You're a lousy researcher." He sucked air. "If we pull up the ladder, they can't get to us."

She hoped the laughter she was hearing was only a trick of the wind, and not Elaine's ghost.

50

The smell of rain was heavy in the air by the time Nick stepped onto the canyon floor. For the moment, the wind had stopped and the dust had settled. The sun dazzled cancerously overhead.

Elliot joined her. Austin was the last one down the rope ladder. The moment his feet hit the ground, Nick led the way, jogging wherever possible. At this point, Boyle's Twist was so narrow they moved in single file, often as not scrambling over boulders that had been washed down from the mountains during past floods.

Nick reached a rockfall she'd nicknamed Boyle's Revenge, where a huge slab of sandstone had sloughed from the cliff, breaking into a ten-foot mound of knife-edged rubble. Scaling it earlier had left her with only a few nicks and abrasions. But now, spurred by the thought of flood, she scrambled for all she was worth. In seconds, her jeans were shredded at the knees and blood was flowing. A fingernail tore to the quick. Behind her, Elliot fell heavily, opening a deep gash in his thigh.

"Keep moving!" he grunted at her.

Nick kept up the breakneck pace until they were within a corkscrew turn of the canyon's entrance. Then she slowed to a creep, hugging the sandstone wall where the shadows were deepest. The others followed close behind, their ragged breath amplified by the narrow fissure. Her own breath sounded just as harsh.

At the last outcropping of rock, she risked a quick peek at their camp. There, fifty yards away in fiery sunlight, two men stood beside a Land Rover. A third lounged in a folding director's chair. All wore wide-brimmed hats and dark glasses. There was something about one of them that made Nick go cold. He had a rifle cradled in his arms, his stance like a big-game hunter who meant business. The other two looked like they'd dressed for the part, safari jackets and tan slacks.

Just as dangerous, though miles away, were the Wasatch Mountains, where black thunderheads rose thirty thousand feet in the air, producing lightning strikes so frequent thunder rumbled like cannon fire.

Nick swallowed sharply. Her Jeep was more than a hundred yards away, with no cover to reach it. Her father's was no closer. They were trapped in Boyle's Twist.

Her only solace was that they probably couldn't see her, standing in sunlight the way they were. Even so, she backed up slowly, praying that her movement didn't catch their eyes.

She breathed words into Austin's ear. "Take a look."

They exchanged places in the ravine. A moment later Austin retreated far enough to whisper, "The one standing, the one without the rifle. His name's Fisher."

"And?" Nick prompted.

"He speaks for the Bishop Foundation and has the power to destroy me. He came to my office two days ago and issued an ultimatum. It wasn't bad enough that they were going to cancel my grant. They upped the ante by threatening to fake data that would prove that I was a plagiarist. That my monograph was another man's work. How can you fight people like that? I had no choice but to cooperate."

"Cooperate?" Nick echoed incredulously. "You sold out. You're a spy."

"Whatever I am, it doesn't matter a damn if we don't get out of here. You saw for yourself. It's raining in the mountains."

"We might survive a flood," Nick replied, "but not a rifle bullet."

"Nobody's going to get killed."

"Will Jennings and Lamar Decker probably said the same thing," she said.

Austin shook his head. "I'll go out and talk to them, explain the situation."

Elliot grabbed his arm. "You're not thinking straight. They know we're archaeologists, not gunmen. So why are they armed?"

Austin wet his lips, his tongue blood-colored from red dust. He saw Nick's reaction and reached out to her. "I'm sorry, Nick."

She backed away from him.

He smiled sadly and said, "Let me do something right, at least."

Then he stepped into the sunlight.

51

A chunk of canyon wall exploded in a hail of sandstone splinters. Nick, who'd been standing closest to Austin, felt a sting. When she touched her check, her hand came away bloody.

"The next shot kills you!" someone shouted.

"I'm alone," Austin called back.

"We know better," the voice said.

Without turning around, Austin flicked his wrist, gesturing at Nick and Elliot to stay back. Where to go was the problem.

"Nicolette Scott!" the voice shouted. "Don't you want to know about Knute and Nora?"

Another voice said, "You, Austin, step out of the canyon."

"Who the hell are you?" Austin bellowed.

"The only ones who know the truth."

"That, I'd like to hear," Nick muttered.

Elliot laid a restraining hand on her shoulder.

"Get to the kiva cave," she told him. "It's a hundred feet up at least, well out of flood range." She remembered the ladder position distinctly. She'd left it coiled on a ledge twenty feet up, within range of their extension ladder. Only the ladder wasn't with them. "A twenty-foot climb and you're home free."

"We'll both go," Elliot said firmly.

She shook her head. "You get there and pull the ladder up after you. And don't lower again for anyone except me or Reed."

"You're crazy."

"With you safe in that cave, we're insured. They're not going to shoot anybody while there's a witness missing. Hell, chances are they aren't going to shoot us anyway," she added, not believing it.

He stared so hard the wrinkles around his eyes quivered. "Knute and Nora aren't worth it."

"Would you say that if someone offered to tell you why the Anasazi disappeared?"

"I'll wait for you right here."

"And do what if I'm wrong, throw rocks?"

52

"That's my rifle," **Nick** said when she got close enough to identify the .30-.30 pointed at her.

"There's no need for that," the man in the director's chair said. "Lower the gun."

The rifleman complied, though he kept the .30-.30 at the ready. The man in the director's chair rose to his feet, smiling. Nick recognized him immediately, a face from the covers of *Newsweek* and *Time*, the man the smart money said would be our next president. Nelson Bishop, philanthropist. An Albert Schweitzer with money. That had been *Time* magazine's description.

She adjusted her Cubs cap and said nothing.

"You're hurt," Bishop said, indicating her cheek. "Get the first-aid kit, Harold."

Harold didn't move. The other

man, the one Austin called Fisher, the one who'd scared him so badly, shook his head as if to say first aid was wasted on the dead.

Bishop must have understood, because he smiled weakly and said, "Maybe later. For now, it's time we introduce ourselves."

"No need," Nick told him.

"This is Paul Fisher," Bishop said anyway. "His publicity campaign has made me a household face. Our friend with the rifle is Harold."

Names were a bad sign. It meant Bishop was confident no one would be around to repeat them.

Over the mountains, lightning intensified, thunder along with it, though in Baptist Wash the heat hadn't abated so much as a degree as far as Nick could tell.

"Now," Bishop continued, "it's time I met your father before we all get wet."

"Knute and Nora first, if you don't mind," Nick said stubbornly.

Harold repositioned the rifle until it was pointing at her kneecap.

"You see how it is," Bishop said.

"My father's in a cave back in the canyon," she said. "When he's with his Anasazi, you can't drag him away."

"She might be telling the truth," Fisher said. "My research says the man's a fanatic on the subject. He's also the recognized expert, though I feel certain Dr. Austin hopes to be next in line for the title."

"Nick," Austin said, his eyes pleading, "I never told him that."

Fisher snickered derisively. "Maybe not in so many words, but he sold you out just the same. Otherwise, we wouldn't be here, would we?"

Bishop overrode him. "Ms. Scott, just tell us where your father is, exactly?"

She gestured toward the canyon's mouth. "Maybe a mile in, maybe a little more."

"I think you'd better show us."

"And Knute and Nora?" she persisted.

"We can talk on the way." Bishop nodded at Fisher, who retrieved a compact Uzi submachine gun from their Land Rover and handed it to Bishop.

Bishop cocked the weapon, then glanced toward the thunderheads engulfing the mountains. "What's the forecast?"

"See for yourself," Nick said. "Those clouds are miles away." And bursting open, she added to herself, just like Kamas.

Bishop looked to Harold, who shrugged and said, "I'm not a local."

"I was born and raised in this country," Austin said abruptly. "There's nothing to worry about. In the heat like this, rain evaporates before it hits the ground." He smiled at Nick tentatively, as if seeking her forgiveness.

Fisher said, "It's always good to have an expert opinion." He snapped his fingers at Harold. "It's time Dr. Austin retired."

Without an instant's hesitation, Harold shot Austin through the head.

The sound of the shot was still echoing when Bishop cut loose with his Uzi. Harold exploded backward, dead before he hit the bloodred ground.

"He shouldn't have done that. Look what he made me do. My God, Fisher, did you see what he made me do?" He threw the gun down in disgust. "I'm not like my father. This is over. Do you understand, Fisher. It's over."

He started to pace up and down. "I could have done great things. I could have been a great man. The country needed me."

"It still does," Fisher insisted. "We can clean this up."

"Clean this up? You mean more killing, more blood on my hands?" He raised his arms and stared at them. "How much blood do I already have on them? It's because of you isn't it, you've entangled me in this web." He charged at Fisher, who shot him before he could take two steps.

"He'd have made a great president," Fisher said. "I guess we're going to have to find someone else."

53

Nick closed her eyes, waiting for the next burst. A jab in the stomach started her breathing again.

"I promised you Knute and Nora, didn't I?" Fisher chuckled. "Besides, I don't think it right a father should outlive his daughter. Lead on. We'll go find him."

Another jab of the Uzi's barrel nudged her on her way.

She smiled to herself and started walking. By not killing her there and then, he'd made a mistake. Now she had a chance. To kill him at least, if not escape herself.

"I'll be right behind you every step of the way," he said.

Good, she thought.

Thunder boomed.

"What about Knute and Nora?" she said to keep his mind off the weather.

"I'll let Bishop's father tell you."

"FDR was our mortal enemy," a tinny voice said.

Nick paused long enough to glance over her shoulder. A palm-sized cassette recorder dangled from a strap around Fisher's wrist.

He gestured with the Uzi and she resumed her pace, accompanied by the voice of Bishop's father. "Roosevelt was taking this country down the road to socialism along with our profits. J. Edgar Hoover was with us on this, though the old bastard was too clever to put anything on paper. 'I'll leave the glory to America's invisible spider,' he said, meaning your grandfather.

"The idea was to discredit FDR, maybe even get him charged with treason. Thinking back on it, I think Hoover knew what the Japanese were up to. Certainly, the Pearl Harbor letters were his idea. To implement them, we set up his longtime friend and college classmate, a banker named Hanover. We looted his bank and made it look like he was stealing the money to finance FDR's re-election campaign."

Nick stumbled, made a grab for an outcropping of rock, missed, and fell to her knees.

Fisher stopped the tape and said, "Get up."

"This all happened over fifty years ago," she spat at him.

He thrust the gun within inches of her face.

"All right," she said, scrabbling to her feet. "I'm walking."

After a few yards, he said, "You're missing the point. This is still going on. The country needs a leader that shares our vision. You don't think that Watergate was really thought up by Nixon, do you? The Eight missed their chance against FDR, but that was their first attempt. The next generation was more successful. Bishop would have been our man. We would have had enough on him before he became president to control him. You've ruined all that."

"Sure."

She rounded a bend and came face-to-face with the rockfall.

"How far is this cave of your father's?" Fisher demanded.

"Just on the other side," she said, pointing at the pile of loose, shrapnellike sandstone. "It's not as bad as it looks."

He gazed at the barrier and shook his head. "You go first. When you're at the top wait for me." He rammed the gun's muzzle against her spine. "Remember, you've got nowhere to run."

She climbed the rockfall like a monkey, using her hands and feet. Halfway up she felt the sandstone tremble beneath her. An instant later, she heard the thunder, sounding closer than ever.

She scrambled to the top. From there, the kiva cave wasn't more than two hundred yards away, albeit two hundred twisting and turning yards. It was now or never.

With all her strength, Nick kicked backward with both feet, sending boulders cascading toward Fisher. Then she threw herself down the other side, landing so hard the breath *whooshed* out of her.

Gasping, she stumbled to her feet and ran for her life. At every step she expected a bullet to smash her spine.

Then she was through the next snakelike twist and the shots were nothing but harmless echoes.

54

On flat ground, Nick could run two hundred yards in half a minute, maybe less. But here? Here was a nightmare of twists and turns.

Behind her Fisher cursed. He sounded close, one twist away, maybe two. Impossible to tell with the wind suddenly howling like an animal.

She ran harder. Youth was on her side, and probably conditioning. Even so, each gasp of breath was painful.

His would be worse. A man out of breath couldn't shoot straight. She hoped.

Suddenly she was through the narrows, with a straightaway leading to the kiva cave. At the sight of it, her heart leaped. The rope ladder hung all the way to the canyon floor. That meant her father was up top already.

She sprinted, the banshee wind at her back.

"Hurry!" Elliot screamed from above.

The rope ladder, almost within grasp, swayed in the gale that was running ahead of the wall of water behind it.

She hurled herself forward like a runner at the finish line.

"Flood!" Elliot shrieked.

Nick lunged for the flailing rope and somehow caught it.

Climb! Her brain screamed.

Her legs, leaden with exhaustion, moved in slow motion. Part of her wanted to look back, to see if the deluge was upon her, rock- and boulder-filled and as deadly as cannon fire. The rest of her knew better than to waste even a second.

She climbed. Each step was like a miracle. No bullet, no cannon shrapnel.

Wind hurled the rope ladder sideways along the canyon wall, dragging her with it. Instinctively, she hooked her arms through the loops and hung on.

At the end of its swing, the ladder slapped her against the stone cliff face. The impact emptied her lungs. A roar filled her head, whether the sound of her own blood or the roar of the onrushing water she didn't know.

For an instant, gunfire overrode the roar. Sandstone exploded in her face. Slivers sliced her cheeks, forehead, and neck.

"Come down or I'll kill you," Fisher shouted.

She tightened her grip on the rope and risked a look. Below, Fisher made a grasp at the flailing rope ladder and missed.

"Bitch!" he screamed, giving up on the ladder to aim at her again.

She thought he pulled the trigger, thought she saw the gun's recoil jolt his body, before the wall of roaring water hit him. After that she could only hang on as the current caught the ladder like so much flotsam, banging it and her against the sandstone wall until Nick's vision narrowed and she was staring into a well. At the bottom of the well, water was rising.

Her feet were cold. Moving them made splashing noises.

She had to climb out of the well, but her hands were snarled in the rope. By force of will, she untangled one, then the other, and moved her feet.

The water was at her knees now, then her waist. The ladder was buffeting relentlessly, banging her into hamburger.

She'd give it one last try and then the hell with it. Reluctantly, one hand released the ladder and stretched as high above her head as she could reach.

No good. She was too tired. She started to sag.

A hand grabbed her wrist. "Goddammit, Nick," Elliot shouted, "don't just stand there. Help me!"

How long it took to reach the cave she had no idea. Her feet must have been working, but she had no memory of it.

After a long time she had breath enough to say, "You saved my life, Elliot."

"There's still a lot of work to be done in this canyon," he said, "so I couldn't afford to lose you."

55

The flood waters receded as quickly as they'd come. One moment they were twenty feet below the kiva cave, rising so quickly Nick felt inundation a certainty, and in the next they were falling away as if a drain hole had opened somewhere.

Steam as thick as smoke rose from the saturated sandstone walls, turning the 100-degree heat into a sauna.

"Before we climb down," Elliot said, "there's something you should see." He unzipped the watertight pocket on the front of his fisherman's vest and extracted a bulky envelope. "I found this when I was hiding the documents in your mother's inner sanctum."

"Why didn't you give it to me when I arrived?" she said.

"You had other things to worry about."

"Do you know what's in it?"

"Yes," he replied abruptly. He retreated to the back of the cave, leaving her some privacy.

She hesitated, the envelope wasn't sealed. Elaine haunted her as it was. Probably she always would. But at least the Elaine Nick envisioned was alive. It had taken Nick years to progress that far, to wipe away the image of finding Elaine's dead body, a suicide, or so the doctor ruled, though no note had been found. Until now. She wanted to throw the envelope away, but her father was waiting.

Elaine had killed herself only hours after having her hair done, the same day she and Nick were scheduled for back-to-back appointments at Shirley's Beauty Salon, the day Nick rebelled and had herself shorn.

Hating the memory, Nick opened the envelope. A single sheet of paper was folded around a wad of red hair, Nick's presumably. No doubt her mother had collected it from Shirley's archrival, Helen's House of Hair, where Nick had done the deed. The paper itself contained a single line in Elaine's handwriting. *You broke my heart.*

"Damn her," Nick muttered, her cave-amplified words bringing Elliot to her side.

"Don't take it personally," he said, producing a letter of his own. It, too, read, *You broke my heart.* "Your mother fed on guilt."

Nick crumpled the note into a ball and would have pitched it over the side except for site management. Instead, she hugged her father. "We're still a family, even if we do have bad memories."

She cursed herself for not having thrown the letters away when she'd found her mother's body. She should have known that her father would eventually find them.

"We have a lot of work ahead of us, if we're going to recover this dig," her father said. "Eventually, we might just be able to prove some interesting cross-cultural ties between the Fremont people and the Anasazi." He always fled to his beloved Anasazi when he couldn't face the pain.

Nick nodded. Dealing with the long dead was so much safer than real life.